Baby Mama's Drama 4
Once a Dog, Always a Dog

A Novel by Lady Lissa

Prologue...

Dominic

Hey there! I bet y'all thought y'all was done with my ass, huh? NOT!

Let me give y'all a recap on how things went down before we get to the real nitty gritty. So, I met this lil chick named Tisha, a real bad ass. The chick was hot! When she told me she was a minor, I was shocked. I had no idea minors were built like brick houses, but there she was. We hung out, it was five of us; me, her, her best friend, Peaches, and my two best buds, Slim and Tory. I liked the chick, so she gave me her number, I hit her up and we started banging on the first night.

Yea, I knew she was only 16 and I was an adult at 21, but pussy didn't have an age, right? Even though she was younger than I was, she still threw that pussy at me, so I took it. I didn't know one man that would have passed up on some good, tight pussy. As a matter of fact, that pussy was so good, it kept me coming back for months. I should have known all good things had to come to an end.

Around the fifth month, I got a phone call. I thought it was Tisha calling to tell me to come over and put it on her. Nah, it was her mom calling from her phone. What kind of shit was that? She said I needed to go over there or she was gonna have me arrested for statutory rape. Now, when she said that, it left me no choice but to go over there. Imagine the shock on my face when Tisha lifted her shirt to show me that she was pregnant. I couldn't say shit, so I shot the gap!

Needless to say, she gave birth to my son and named him D.J., short for Dominic Junior. As if that wasn't enough, I met this chick named Rasheeda. She was a little bit thicker than the chicks I usually fucked with, but she had a fat ass. I'm an ass man all day, every day, so of course, I tried to get with that. It took a little persuasion, but she also let me hit within that week. But Lawd have mercy, she didn't use any birth control either. She popped up pregnant a few months later, gave birth to our daughter, Arianna.

So, Tisha hit me up to go visit our son when he was about three months old. Since her mom wasn't around, I figured I'd go see my lil dude. Why she came to the door with some lil bitty ass shorts that was cutting her damn twat and shit? Tisha looked sexy as fuck! Her boobs had gotten bigger, her hips had spread a little and she was thick in all the right places. My tongue hit the floor like a dog on a hot summer's day. She went to get our son, who looked just like me by the way, and I held him and fed him. He fell back to sleep, so she went to put him in the bed. Soon as she entered the room, I was all over her. I couldn't help myself.

I got in that pussy, right there on her mama's couch and busted that thang wide open. The whole time I was hitting it, she was talking about how much she loved me. That was the last thing I wanted to hear. All I wanted to do was bust that nut and keep it moving. Anyway, she got pregnant from that little tryst between us. I was offshore for four months and when I came back, that was the news I received…Tisha was pregnant by me with twins! I was really tossing back the alcohol then.

Five months later, she gave birth to twin girls, but not before she took my ass to child support court. I couldn't believe the judge had the nerve to make me pay almost $800. Where was the justice in that shit?

So far, I had four kids...well, five if you counted my daughter I had with Trina. Trina and I had fucked around a long time ago. The only time I went by there was for sex every once in a while. How come I show up there one night and Tisha's there? As it turned out, the two of them were roommates. Go figure.

Oh yea! I even got shot and the police still didn't know who did it. Then, I met this chick at the gas station who invited me to her place. She had heard some shit about my good dick and wanted to find out if it was true. I was more than happy to give it to her. BOOM! Fucked her squealing ass and she popped up pregnant. Now that was some bullshit! It was crazy because I didn't even need a DNA tests for any of my kids. They all looked like me because of my strong ass genes. I was in denial though. I didn't want to admit that I had fathered all those kids.

Anyway, Mariah gave birth to my daughter and put me on child support too. I left and went offshore. It was way too much drama going on for me. Got offshore and met this chick named Rochelle. She was fine as fuck, but scared of being on the water. She allowed me to hold and comfort her for two months before we finally got busy. I wished I had kept my dick in my draws.

A few months later, she called and told me that she was pregnant. Damn! Oh, I forgot to mention that I slept with my best friend, Tory's girl once. She turned up pregnant with twins, one for him and one for me. What the fuck was up with that? He and I fell out behind that shit. That nigga beat my ass and hers. I deserved that shit though because I had crossed a line. We were brothers and I should've never fucked over my boy that way.

On top of all the shit that was going on with all these babies, Rochelle had a girl by the way, I met April. She wanted nothing to do with me at all. I chased that girl until she finally agreed to go out with me. I knew I shocked a lot of people when I started dating April because she was white, but hell, she was the only one that made me chase her. Everyone else just gave me the pussy with no problem. Who knew that I would actually enjoy chasing the pussy? I didn't.

Things were going great and that was when tragedy struck. My boy, Slim and his girl, Peaches were killed inside their home. I couldn't believe that shit and it struck me hard. Slim was one of my best friends, we were more like brothers. He had been trying his best to get me to act right and take care of my kids, but I couldn't do it. But once I lost my friend, I realized that life was too short to be petty. It was time for me to grow the hell up and start taking responsibility for my shit.

So, I decided to make peace with my babies' mamas and get to know my kids. I had a big party for them and they all got along. I proposed to April and she finally gave me some pussy. I didn't forget about the two murders I committed, I just tried not to think about them. I had been helping my mom with my little sister ever since she was born. We didn't speak about her dad at all because we didn't want to think about the bad memories that came with it.

So, I think I gave the 4-1-1 on everything. I was now an engaged man with eight kids. I still worked offshore in a supervisor's position and still support all my kids. But why did I have to be the one that drama continued to follow. A nigga was trying to change, but people wouldn't let me.

Now that y'all caught up, follow me as I take you through my life once again…

Chapter one

Dominic

Six months later...

"Mmmmm!" April moaned as I drove my dick inside her. That girl had taught me a lot since we had been together. Throughout all my shit, she stuck by me.

We were positioned on our sides and I had her left leg up as I continued to plow into her from behind. She was throwing her pussy at me and I was taking everything she had. I never knew how to love until I met April. She made me chase her like I never had to do with other chicks. That was what made her special. Any other chick would've fallen in my bed by the third or fourth time I made a pass at them. Not April.

Shit, it took almost six months after I met her before she even agreed to go out on a date with me. "Oh my God!" April cried out as her body trembled. I knew she was having an orgasm.

"Roll over, ma," I said. She rolled onto her stomach as I got behind her. I positioned myself behind her as she got on all fours. She arched her back as I prepared to plow into her. I plunged into her and she cried out.

I held her hips as I plowed my dick into her. Her sexy ass bounced against my pelvis, turning me on even more. As I continued to beat that pussy up, she moaned in pleasure. I finally hit her with that one last thrust as we both shuddered from the intensity of the orgasm. I laid beside her for a couple of seconds before I climbed out of the bed and headed to the bathroom. I removed the used condom and flushed it down the toilet. I cleaned off my dick and made my way back to the bedroom.

By the time I had made it back to the bedroom, April was already up and about. "Where you going?" I asked.

"I'm going over to Sheila's so we could go over some wedding stuff," she said with a smile.

Lately, every time I heard her talking about the wedding, my palms began to sweat, and my nerves got bad as fuck. I didn't know why that kept happening to me. I loved April and I proposed to her because I wanted to marry her. At least that was what I thought I wanted.

"What's wrong with you?" she asked.

"What you talkin' bout?" I asked.

"I mean, why did you make that face when I mentioned wedding stuff? Are you having cold feet?"

"What face?"

"That grimace?"

"Oh, I didn't even notice dat I had done anything. Nah, I ain't gettin' cold feet." At least, I hoped I wasn't. I ain't never been married before, but I thought it was what I wanted. I mean, wasn't that what men wanted when they got older; to be married to the woman they loved and build a life together. I didn't know why I was getting so antsy these days.

"Are you sure? I mean, the wedding is in six months. The last thing I want is for you to leave me at the altar," she said, her face taking on a serious expression.

"I wouldn't leave you at da altar, babe. I'm good," I said.

"Okay." She slipped her feet in her flip flops and asked, "What are you gonna do while I'm gone?"

"I guess I'ma hit up Tory and see if he wants to hang out. Maybe hit up Bourbon or something," I said.

"Okay. Well, I'll see you later," she said as she walked over and gave me a kiss.

"Aight."

After she left, I grabbed my phone and hit up Tory.

"S'up bro?"

"Aye, whatchu got going on? You feel like hanging out?"

"Whatchu got in mind?" he asked.

"I'on know. April going over wedding shit with Sheila, so I'm tryna ta get out of the house. You wanna go on da Riverwalk or something?" I asked.

"Yea, aight. You wanna scoop me up or you want me ta come roll thru?"

"I'ma come thru. Gimme about an hour or so," I said.

"Aight, cool."

We ended the call and I hopped in the shower. When I was done, I hopped out and dried myself off. I made my way into the bedroom and to the closet. Once I was dressed, I grabbed my keys and headed out the door.

*****

30 minutes later, I pulled up to Tory and Ashley's place. I parked my car and got out. I wanted to see my son before we left. Kyon had gotten so big and I felt bad that I had missed the first few months of his life. He and his brother had just celebrated their second birthdays. When I walked in the house, he came running up to me. I scooped him up and gave him a hug.

"Wassup lil man?" I asked as I kissed his cheek.

"Dadeee!" he squealed happily. Keenan came over to me and I scooped him up also.

"Dang, y'all some heavy lil butts," I said as I smiled at them.

"S'up man?" Tory greeted me.

"S'up bro, you ready ta go?" I asked.

"Yep."

I put the kids down and told Kyon, "Daddy gon' be back ta see you soon, okay?"

He began to whine when he saw me leaving, so Ashley came and got him. As I walked out the door with Tory, I could hear him calling for me. I felt bad about leaving him, but I promised myself that I'd get him to come spend the night with me later.

"So, how's it going?" Tory asked me once we were on our way.

"Making it do what it do, ya know?"

"How's the wedding plans going?"

I didn't know why he was asking me about that. I mean, I didn't wanna hear that shit coming from April, so I definitely didn't want to hear it from him now. I mean, I was happy that I had April. She was an amazing girlfriend. I actually had fallen in love with her. When I asked her to marry me, I thought I had reacted too quickly. I think I should've thought that shit out a little more. I was just so happy to have found a chick that had captured my attention that way. I hadn't even gotten the pussy from her until six months into our relationship. I had to beg her to date me for almost six months, mostly because I spent a lot of that time offshore. Then, I couldn't get the pussy until six months after we started dating. It was cool though. I didn't mind waiting.

But I should have waited on that proposal though.

"Uh, can we talk about something else? I mean, I hear April talking about wedding dis, wedding dat all day long. I'd just like ta chill with my bro without thinking about da wedding. Can we do dat?" I asked.

"Yea, aight. What's da matter though? You gettin' cold feet?" he asked.

"Why I gotta have cold feet cuz I don't wanna talk about da wedding?"

"Aye, I'm just asking. I thought you were excited about marrying April."

"Yea, I thought so too."

"Now you don't think so?" he asked, looking at me with a confused look on his face.

"I'on know. Sometimes, I think maybe I rushed dis engagement. Like, maybe I shouldn't have asked so soon. Ya know I was reeling off of Slim's death and shit. I just...I'on know," I said.

"So, whatchu gon' do?"

"I'on know what the fuck I'm gon' do."

I pulled onto Canal Street and he asked, "What, we finna go on Bourbon?"

"Yea, I need ta get some alcohol in my system and think about dis shit. I don't wanna hurt nobody, especially not April. I just think dat maybe we rushing into dis marriage thing, ya know?" I asked.

"Yea, I know. Ashley keep trying ta get me ta marry her, but I can't do it. I just can't get over da fact dat she had a baby by you. I know dat she apologized and shit. I forgave her ass, but I just can't forget. Da fact dat she told you I had gone ta the store and would be back soon. Da fact dat she allowed you ta wait knowing dat I was at work meant dat she had something planned all along. Dat kind of betrayal, I just can't deal with it," he said.

I felt bad about the part I played in the demise of his relationship with Ashley. I hated that I allowed her to seduce me that way. Tory was my boy and for that reason alone I should have never crossed that line. I didn't know why I allowed my dick to get me in that situation. But he was right. She invited me in knowing that man was at work and wouldn't be coming home any time soon. She wore those little cut her ass short shorts and sucked my dick.

We exited the car and started walking. It never ceased to amaze me how any time of the day you could walk down Bourbon Street and it was all the way live. We stopped at the daiquiri shop and got each a daiquiri with some extra shots. As we rounded the corner, I heard someone calling my name.

"DOMINIC!" I continued walking. I wasn't sure who she was or why she was calling me, but the last thing I needed was another woman in my life. "DOMINIC"

"Aye, some chick calling yo name back there," Tory said.

"Yea, well, I don't give a shit. All women do is get my ass caught up in some more shit," I said.

"We been through dat shit already, bro. You've accepted your responsibility in getting them pregnant, so let's not go backwards."

"Yea, but I'm not gonna worry about whoever is calling my name."

"DOMINIC! DOMINIC!"

"Keep walking, man," I said.

I felt someone pulling on my shirt. "Dominic, I know you heard me calling you," the chick said when she finally caught up to us. I turned around to see who was pulling on my jacket. The chick was a red headed, light skinned bad ass. I wondered who the fuck she was and why she was trying so hard to get my damn attention.

"Do I know you?" I asked. Shit, I was confused as a muthafucka. I had never seen this chick before.

"Really Dom? You really gonna act like you don't know me right now?" she asked.

I looked at Tory and he said, "Don't look at me, nigga."

"Dom, are you serious?"

"I'm sorry, but I think you might have the wrong Dominic," I said.

"No, I have the right one. What I'm trying to figure out is how come you playin' me right na," she said.

"I'm playin' you. I don't even know you!"

"Dominic, I met you four years ago. We actually had a relationship dat lasted for about six months," she said.

"So, we had a relationship for six months?"

"Yes."

"Nah, if we had a relationship for six months four years ago, I'd remember," I said.

She pulled out her phone and ran her finger up and down the screen for several minutes. She turned the phone and thrust it in my face. I stared at the pic she was showing me. The chick in the pic did look familiar, but instead of red hair, she had black hair with purple highlights. I was wracking my brain trying to remember her. Then it hit me.

"Shawna?" I asked. "Is your name Shawna?"

"Yes, now all of a sudden you remember me, huh?"

Hell yea, I remembered her. She and I was fucking hot and heavy back in the day. Damn. I had forgotten all about her ass. "Yea, I remember. We wasn't in no relationship though."

"No? Well, what would you call it?"

"I'd call it for what it was… a fuckship."

"What?!"

"We had a fuckship. We was just two people who like ta fuck fuckin' around. Anyway, how you been?"

My eyes roamed from her face to her chest down to her flat stomach, nice waistline and thick thighs. She had put on a little weight since the last time I saw her, but she was still fine as fuck. "I've been good. How about you?" she asked.

"I'm straight. This my bro, Tory," I said.

"Nice to meet you," she told Tory. He just nodded his head in her direction. "I think you and I need to have a talk."

"About?"

"It's personal."

"Anything you gotta say, you can say in front of Tory," I said. I hadn't seen this chick in years. I doubted if anything she had to tell me required that much privacy.

"We need to talk about our son," she said.

"Our son?" I asked.

"Yea, did you forget about our little boy?"

"Forget? I didn't know shit about you having a little boy. Even if I did, I sure didn't know dat kid was mine!" I said. What the fuck was she trying to pull?

"So, when I told you that I was pregnant, what'd you think? That I was gonna put him up for adoption or something?"

"Wait, hold up. I don't even remember you tellin' me shit about a baby!" I said. This girl must be delusional or something.

Bitches was steady trying to pin babies on me. I knew damn well I wasn't the only nigga in the New Orleans area with a dick. What I couldn't understand was why they kept pointing the finger at me. I wasn't the only nigga out here fucking.

"Dom, I called you as soon as I found out I was pregnant. You were offshore and were supposed to contact me when you got back," she said.

Now, I knew damn well she was telling a bold faced lie. Anyone who knew me back then knew that I didn't want to be no daddy. It took for my boy Slim to get killed for me to grow the hell up for my kids. I would've never told her I'd call her back. I would've hung up on her ass so fast, she would've thought she had called Superman instead of Dominic Williams.

"You ain't never told me no shit like dat!" I said.

"I know I did. Anyway, you wanna see your son or not? I mean, you've been absent from his life for three years. You wanna make it to four?" she asked.

"How do I know dats my kid? How do I know you ain't trying to pin somebody else's kid on me?"

She scrolled through her phone and pulled up another pic. She turned it for me to see and it was a pic of her son. HER son. I didn't know who that kid's father was, but it sure wasn't me. That little boy looked like he could belong to the milk man, but definitely not me. You could tell he was a boy that was mixed with black and white. He wasn't an all-black kid, so he definitely wasn't mine. He didn't even look like me or my kids and all my kids resembled me.

"That ain't ma kid," I said.

"WHAT?! He looks just like you!"

"You heard me." I looked at Tory and he had an unsure look on his face. "C'mon bro, you know dat ain't my kid. All my kids look just like me. Dis one looks like a white man's kid."

WHAP!

"Don't you fuckin' try to play me like that!" she growled. "Why the hell would I tell you my baby was yours if he wasn't? Don't nobody got time for games like that!"

Now, the old me, would've snatched her up by her weave and popped the shit out of her. But the me I was now, wasn't about to do that shit, especially not in public where I could get my ass locked up.

"Is everything alright over here?" a police officer asked.

"Yea, we straight," I responded. "Let's go, man," I told Tory.

"When are you gonna come see your son?" Shawna asked.

"Yo, it was almost nice seeing you again, but you need to go find your real baby's daddy. Don't put dat shit on me! Ya heard me?"

With that being said, I walked away. There was no way I was going to admit that kid was mine. I heard her screaming my name and calling me a deadbeat as Tory and I walked away. I didn't care what the fuck she said about me, I knew that I wasn't the same dude I once was. I was ten times better than who I used to be. I was a good father, but I wasn't about to claim a kid that wasn't my kid. I already had eight and that was enough for me right now.

"Yo, you sure dat ain't yo kid?" Tory asked.

I stopped walking to look at him. "Did you see da same kid dat I saw?"

"Yea, but his mom is light skinned, so maybe the kid took after her. I'm just sayin', you might wanna to take a DNA test."

"Fuck dat! I got eight kids already! Eight fuckin' kids! I don't need another one," I said.

"Even if he might be yours?" he asked. "I mean, he did resemble you a little."

"Nigga, whose side are you on?"

"I'm on the kid's side. I mean, he needs his father, man. A girl can be raised by just her mom, but a boy needs his dad."

"Look bro, can we just concentrate on having a good time? I mean, ain't dat what we came here for?"

"Yea, you're right. I won't say another word about it," Tory said.

"Good." The two of us walked down Bourbon for the next couple of hours, all thoughts of Shawna and her son gone from my mind.

Chapter two

Tisha

I woke up to the smell of bacon coming from the kitchen. I knew that Reggie was cooking breakfast. I looked at my phone to see what time it was. It was almost nine in the morning. I couldn't believe that he had let me sleep in again. That man was so good to me. I kept thinking that I was sleeping and that I'd wake up and realize that this thing with Reggie was all a dream. But, after being with this wonderful man for almost two years, I had to accept the fact that it wasn't a dream and he really had chosen me. I made my way to the bathroom, so I could pee and take care of my hygiene.

I threw my robe on and followed the smell to the kitchen. Sure enough, he was standing at the stove, cooking breakfast. The kids were sitting in front of the television watching Paw Patrol.

"Mommy! Mommy!" D.J. said as he came running to give me a hug. The girls followed behind him, their little chubby cheeks wide from smiling. I reached down and hugged them all.

"Hey babies, what are y'all doing?" I asked.

"Watching TV," D.J. said. My little boy had gotten so big. He was almost three years old already. It was hard to believe that I was 19 years old with three kids, but that was the reality of my situation.

"Hey baby," Reggie greeted.

"Hey babe," I said.

I watched as he placed the three small plates on the kid's table. "Come eat guys," he called to them. The three of them took off running like a small pack of hungry wolves. I smiled as they put their little butts in the chairs.

I walked over to Reggie and wrapped my arms around his neck. "Thanks for cooking breakfast," I said as I kissed him. He kissed me back, shoving his tongue in my mouth.

"Mmmm! Dats what I'm talkin' bout!" he said as our kiss ended. "You know you don't have to thank me for cooking. I'm always happy to help out."

"Don't you work today?" I asked.

"Yep, I'ma go in this afternoon at one. You were sleeping so peacefully, I didn't want to wake you. So, I got the kids dressed and fixed breakfast."

"You should've woken me up, baby. I don't like when I'm the reason you have to go in to work later," I said.

"I don't mind. Lemme fix you a plate," he said and released me. He walked back into the kitchen and returned with two plates of food. He grabbed two glasses of orange juice and we sat down to eat. I couldn't thank God enough for this man. He had broken the bank when he made Reggie. He was such a wonderful man to me and my kids.

"Have you heard from Dom lately?" he asked.

"Not since the last time he was here to see the kids," I responded. I didn't know what was going on with him lately. He was better as a father to the kids than he was in the beginning, but lately, he had been shirking on his duties. It had been almost two months since the kids had seen him. That was another reason that I was so thankful for Reggie.

"Damn. Dats been about two months, huh?" Reggie asked.

"Yep."

"Have you called him?"

"Babe, now you know if I had spoken to him, I'd tell you. I see no need to call him. I mean, he knows he has kids here, so it's up to him to come see them," I said.

I knew Reg felt a little insecure at times because of my history with Dom, but he had no reason to feel such a way. I was never going to fall back into bed with Dom.

"You know I love you, right?" I asked as I looked up at him.

"Yea, I know. I love you too, babe. I also love the family that we've made. You know what I wish though?"

"What?"

"I wish that you had a baby by me," he said.

I rolled my eyes because this wasn't a conversation that I wanted to have. We had discussed this quite a few times already. I didn't want anymore kids right now. Three was too many as it was, and as much as I loved my babies, I wished I had slowed down on having them back to back. The one good thing about that was they had each other to play with.

"Babe, I know you want to have a baby with me, but I'm just not ready," I said.

"I know. I don't want to pressure you either."

"I appreciate that, but when you keep telling me how bad you want a baby with me, it feels like pressure," I said.

"I never want to pressure you into doing anything you don't want to do. I love you so much, Tisha. I just don't know what else to do to prove that to you," he said.

"There's nothing else you can do. I know that you love me. I just don't think that you understand how much I went through before we met."

The kids finished eating and went back to watch television. "I know how much you went through, babe. Trust me when I tell you that you'll never have to worry about me walking away from my responsibilities," he said.

"How do I know that you won't just up and leave me?"

"Wow! Really, bae? You really gonna keep asking me dat like I'm dat nigga?"

"Yes!"

"Well, I'm gonna go get dressed for work," he said.

"What? So, you're just going to walk away, huh?"

"It just makes no sense for us to keep having dis conversation. I love you and I thought you knew dat. But apparently, you're still comparing me to your baby's daddy. So, I'm gonna just go to work because I don't want to say something dat I'll regret later," he said.

As he disappeared into the bedroom, I followed behind him. I wasn't done talking about this, even though it was clear that he was. I just couldn't understand why we continued to argue about this shit. I loved Reggie, don't get me wrong. I just wasn't ready to have any more kids right now. I was still in school and even though I was working, it was hard to believe that I had three kids and I wasn't even legal age to buy alcohol yet. What would I do with four or five kids if things didn't work out between Reggie and I? I wasn't going back on Section 8 again. I liked being able to afford my own place to stay. Of course, Reggie paid the rent, but I contributed to the other bills.

I just didn't want to go back on government assistance again. If I had more kids, that was exactly what was going to happen.

"Why are you so upset? I mean, you should understand why I don't want to have any more kids right now. I'm only 19 years old and I have three babies under four years old. D. J. is only two and a half and the girls just turned 18 months. How can you expect me to be so ready to have more kids?" I asked.

"Tisha, I said I didn't wanna discuss it anymore. I understand where you're coming from, but dat don't mean I still don't want kids because you ain't ready," he said.

"So, what does dat mean? Dat you're going to go make kids with somebody else?"

"Did I say dat shit? All I said was just because you ain't ready, don't mean I don't want kids. Look, I love your kids. I love them just as if they are my own…"

"So, what's the problem?"

"The problem is dat they ain't my biological kids! I want my own kids, Tee Tee!" he said.

I didn't know if he was trying to hurt me or not, but he was. I shouldn't have come into the room. I should've let him just walk away, but I didn't. Now, I was standing here listening to him tell me that he loved my kids, but they weren't his kids. I knew that without him telling me that. He didn't have to say that to me. He only needed to tell me that he wanted kids. He didn't have to hurt me that way.

I stood there with my mouth open and tears welling up in my eyes, but I wasn't going to cry. "Okay Reg," I said softly as I turned around. I wasn't going to argue with him anymore.

I knew that my kids weren't his biological kids. I guess I was just fooling myself into thinking that he could be happy with the four of us. My kids knew that Dom was their dad, but they thought Reggie was their dad too. After all, he was the only dad they knew for a long time. Reggie had stepped up for them when Dom didn't want to and for that, I'd always be grateful. But right now, at this moment, my heart was breaking. I felt like he was about to break up with me and that wasn't a good feeling.

"This the reason I didn't wanna discuss this no more. I don't want to hurt your feelings or make you cry," he said.

"I'm okay," I said, not bothering to turn and look at him.

"Nah, you ain't okay. But I gotta get to work," he said. He kissed me on the lips and walked away. I watched as he gave the kids a hug, grabbed his keys and walked out. I was left standing there, wishing we had never started this conversation. As much as I loved Reggie, I didn't know why he was so adamant about the two of us having a baby.

I just needed him to understand that now wasn't the time…

Chapter three

Rasheeda

Things didn't quite work out between Charles and I. Charles was sweet, dependable and he treated my baby girl so good. But even though he was all those things, I still couldn't be with him. For some reason, I couldn't get Dominic and what he had put me through out of my head. I didn't want to care about Dom the way that I did, but I couldn't help it. When he came by to visit our daughter, it took everything in me to keep my hands off of him. He always looked and smelled so good.

I hated that he was with that white girl, April. It wasn't that I was prejudice or anything against white people, but why did she have to have him. I mean, out of all the black women they had in the New Orleans area, why did a white girl have to get another one of our black men? And why did it have to be my baby's daddy? I probably wouldn't have tripped so much if he had chosen to be with Tisha. After all, she did have three kids with him. But from what I understood, Tisha was very happy without him.

Her man, Reggie was fine, so I could definitely understand why he had stolen her heart. Also, when Dom had the party for all his baby mamas and children to meet, I saw how Reggie was interacting with her kids. He was really good and patient with them. He actually treated them as if they were his own kids. I had no idea that he had a child with Reggie's sister. That was his little well-kept secret I guess.

I didn't want anyone to think I was a straight fool because I wasn't. I remembered every single thing that

Dominic did to hurt me. I remembered every lie he ever told me, so I'd never want to go back to those times again. But the Dominic that I knew now wasn't the same one that he was back then. He was changed and different. He still looked just as handsome as ever, but he was still different. I guess you could say he grew up. It was too bad that it took for his best friend to get killed for him to step it up as a father. I knew that had hit him hard. Not only had he told me about it, but he had cried on my shoulder a couple of times. It never went further than me comforting my daughter's daddy, but if it had, I wouldn't have minded.

Currently, it had been about a month since Arianna had seen her daddy. I had called him a couple of times, but he blew me off. He said when he had time, he'd come around. I knew it was because of that white girl that he hadn't been around, and for that reason, I had no respect for her ass. What woman would want to keep a man away from his kids? If she was the angel he claimed she was, she would have encouraged him to visit Arianna. I had a feeling she didn't like him coming over here. That was all good because I offered to meet him at the park or even at his mom's house.

I loved his mom. Ms. Belinda was a doll and I often brought Arianna over there to play with her auntie. That was funny to say. Arianna had an auntie that was younger than she was, but she loved to play with Nina. As a matter of fact, I was going to call Ms. Belinda and see if we could go visit today. Maybe, we'd be lucky enough to run into Dom while we were there.

"Hello," she answered on the second ring.

"Ms. Belinda, were you asleep? I'm sorry if you were. I didn't mean to disturb you," I quickly apologized.

"No, it's okay, Rasheeda. I'm just a little worn out from this little girl is all. How's it going?" she asked.

"It's going okay. I was just wondering if Arianna and I can come by for a little while. Ari is missing her little auntie."

"Oh, well, yea. Y'all can come by in about an hour. Dat way when you guys leave, I can put Nina down for her nap and take one of my own."

"Okay, well, we'll get ready and be over there soon," I said.

"Okay, see y'all then."

We ended the call and I went to get my baby girl ready to leave. She had gotten so big over these last few months. She had just turned two last month, so she was at that terrible two stage. You know, the one that got into every single thing even when I said no. She also whined and cried every time I told her no for something. Those were the times when I think she missed her daddy. Those were the times when I wished that Dom and I had worked things out.

*****

An hour and 15 minutes later, I was parking my car in Ms. Belinda's driveway. I opened the back door and reached for my little bad girl. She was so happy that we were here, she couldn't stop smiling. I knocked on the door and Ms. Belinda opened it with Nina in tow. She squealed with joy when she saw Arianna and so did my little girl.

"Y'all come on in," Ms. Belinda said.

We walked in and gave her a hug. "Hey, Ms. Belinda," I greeted.

I placed Arianna on the floor and she took off for Nina. The two of them walked over to Nina's toys and began to play on the floor. "Hey baby," she said.

I couldn't help but notice that she had lost a little weight. She actually looked really worn out. "Ms. Belinda, are you sure you're feeling okay?" I asked after taking in her condition.

"Yea, I'm fine. I told you dat dis little girl has been wearing me out. I had no idea what I was getting myself into by having another baby at my age," she said.

"I can only imagine. I mean, you have a 24-year old and a one year old. You basically started all over again."

"You telling me. I'm gonna have to get me some vitamins just so I can keep my energy level up," she said.

"I know dats right. Other than being tired, how've you been?"

"I've been real good. It's hard raising a child by yourself, which I shouldn't have to tell you. I know dat even though you and Dom are on good terms, he still works a lot, so he barely gets to see the baby," she said.

"Yea, if dats the real reason," I said.

"Whatchu mean? Dom ain't the same way he used to be, you know dat. He's been taking care of all his kids."

"No, you're right, he's not the same as he used to be. But can I be honest with you?" I knew I needed to tread lightly with this because even though Ms. Belinda and I were cool, Dom was still her son. I didn't want to do or say anything that would cause us to argue.

"Yea, what's up?"

"Well, Dom hasn't been by to visit Ari for about a month. Did he leave to go back offshore yet?" I asked, even though I knew that wasn't the case.

"No, he doesn't leave until next Tuesday," she said.

Next Tuesday was four days from now, but I knew I wouldn't see him before he left. He had been avoiding us for some reason.

"Well, I don't know why he wouldn't come see the baby. Unless, dat woman is keeping him from Arianna and I pray dat ain't the reason. I don't wanna have to kick her where the sun don't shine," I said.

"I don't think it has anything to do with April. She knows about his kids and hell, she still agreed to marry him. I think it's just dat they been busy planning their wedding. You know they getting married in six months, right?" she asked.

No, I didn't know. I knew he had proposed to her, which I was still trying to wrap my brain around. But now, they were planning to get married in six months. What the hell?! Why would he wanna get married so soon?

"Is she pregnant?" I asked Ms. Belinda, giving her the side eye.

"No, not dat I know of." Her phone began to ring, so she held up her hand. "Dats Dom calling right now," she said. I didn't know why, but my heart skipped a beat when she told me he was on the phone. "Hey baby," she answered.

There was a slight pause before she began speaking again. "I was just sitting her talking to Rasheeda and watching the girls play." Another pause. "Yea, she came by because Ari was missing Nina. You should've seen how happy dey was to see each other."

She paused as she listened. Then she said, "Okay, we'll see you in a bit."

Oh shit! My heart and pussy was about to bust through the ceiling. Dom was coming over here. I couldn't believe I still had these strong feelings for him. I guessed I was really in love with him and until I was able to get him completely out of my system, I'd always feel this way.

"Dom said he gon' come over and see us in a bit."

"Oh yea? Well, that's good," I said, hoping she couldn't tell how happy I was. Of course, I was happy that my daughter was going to be able to see her daddy. But I was glad that I'd get to see him too.

"Don't act like you ain't happy he coming over here," she said.

"Ms. Belinda, what you talkin' bout?"

"Mmm hmm," she said.

"Ari, your daddy is coming by to see you, baby!" I said.

"Yaayyy!"

I was glad my baby was happy. If she only knew how happy I was. Although, I wasn't too happy to hear that

Dom and that chick would be married six months from now. About 20 minutes later, I heard the booming sound of his stereo system bumping in the driveway. He turned the car off and walked in a couple of minutes later.

"Dayeeee!" Ari hollered as she and Nina ran to hug Dom.

"Hey, hey!" He smiled happily as he scooped them both up. He kissed them on their cheeks as they giggled happily. He walked over to the chair where his mom was sitting and gave her a kiss on the cheek. He walked over to the sofa where I was sitting and sat down next to me. I inhaled his intoxicating scent of my favorite cologne, Polo Black.

"S'up, Rah," he said.

"Chillin' Dom," I retorted.

"Whatchu doing over here?" he asked me.

"Ari wanted to come play with Nina." He placed the two girls on their feet and they ran to the toys.

"Oh," he said as he turned his attention to his mom. "Ma, you aight?"

"Yea, just a little tired," Ms. Belinda said.

"You need to get you some vitamins," he said. "I been telling you dat you need dat shit. You ain't the spring chicken you used to be."

"I was just telling Rasheeda the same thing. I just ain't had a chance to go to da store yet," his mom said.

"I'ma getchu some from the Walgreen's up da street when I leave," Dom said.

"Well, if you get it when you leave, dat ain't gon' do me no good," Ms. Belinda said.

"Well duh, ma! I'ma bring it ta you before I go home," he said as he shook his head.

"Thank you, baby," she said.

"You know what? If you wanna take a nap, I'ma be here for a bit," Dom offered.

"You sure?"

"Yea, mom. Go getchu some rest."

"Thank you, baby. I'll only lie down for a couple of hours," she said.

"It's cool," he said.

She got up from the chair and made her way to her bedroom. She closed the door and Dom turned his attention to me. "You looking good, Rah. You been working out or something?"

"Yea, I do have a two year old, ya know? She keeps me super busy," I said. I was glad that he noticed my weight loss. I had worked hard to lose those last 20 pounds. I weighed 230 when I had Arianna and then, I had gotten pregnant again with my baby boy. But, over the past year, I decided to start eating healthier and exercising. I guess you could say that the comments about my fat ass had me feeling some kind of way.

I was happy to say that I was now down to 173 and sexier than I had ever been. So, when Dom complimented me, I knew he meant it. I knew for a fact that I looked good.

"Well, whatever you been doing is working out damn good for you," he said as he checked me out. I actually had a smaller waistline than when he and I first met. Thank God, I still had my big fine ass though.

"So, your mom tells me dat your wedding is in six months," I said.

"Yep." I could tell immediately that his body had tensed up.

"Are you ready for dat? I mean, to be married and all."

"I guess."

"You guess? Shouldn't you be sure before you jump the broom? I mean, dats a huge step, especially for you," I said.

"Yea, I know. Anyway, how are you and what's his name?" he asked.

"Really, Dom?"

"What?!" he asked with a confused expression on his face.

"So, you don't remember me telling you dat we broke up?"

"Nah, when you told me dat?"

"Uh, about six months ago."

"Shit, I don't remember that shit. What happened?" he asked.

"Nothing. I just wasn't ready for what he was ready for," I said.

"And what was dat?"

"Whatever it was, I just wasn't ready, okay?"

"Aight."

"So, are you ready?"

"I said yea," he said.

"No, what you said was you guess," I said.

"Why you keep asking me dat shit? I didn't come here so you could bother me about my wedding plans," he said. I could tell he was getting aggravated, so I decided to let it be.

"Sorry. I was just making sure dat you were ready."

"Why does it matter so much to you?"

"Because she's going to be my daughter's stepmother, dats why."

I couldn't believe he would even ask me that. Of course, I would care if he married someone else. Whoever he did marry would be associated with my child. I didn't let her go over there yet because I didn't trust that woman. I didn't know what it was about her, but something wasn't right.

"Well, trust me, I wouldn't be marrying her if I thought she wasn't a good role model," he said.

"So, why haven't you been by to see Ari? I mean, you were doing so well. What happened to make you not come by to see your baby in almost a month?" I asked.

"Uh, you do know dat I have seven other kids, right?"

"What dat mean? You laid down and made them, so dat shouldn't be your excuse why you can't visit them," I said.

"I guess I was just busy. We've been planning the wedding, plus I've been working. This new job ain't no shit. I told you dat a few times before."

"Yea, I know. But your baby misses you."

"She ain't even worried about me right nah. I think you da one be missin' me," he said.

Shit, he got that right. I was missing him and his dick, but I wasn't about to tell him that though. I looked at the time and realized that we had been here for two hours. Luckily for me, I was off today.

"Well, I'm gonna get Ari and get out of your hair. I promised to take her to the park." I stood up and called over to Ari. "Ari, come hug and kiss your daddy bye bye."

"Noooo!" she cried. I knew it was going to be a hassle to get her out of the house. I looked at Dom to see what he was going to do. He stood up and walked over to Arianna and Nina.

"Ari, your mom is ready ta go. She said she was gon' take you ta da park. You don't wanna go ta da park?" he asked her.

She dried her eyes and nodded her head. "Well, if you wanna go ta da park, you gotta go with mommy. Daddy and Nina gon' see you soon." Dom reached for her and she stepped into his open arms. He held her close as Nina watched. She looked a little sad that her playmate was leaving, but I was sure that Dom would keep her entertained until her mom woke from her nap. He picked Ari up and asked her for a kiss. She kissed and hugged her daddy before he handed her over to me.

"Thank you," I said as Ari put her head on my shoulder.

"No problem," he said as he picked up Nina and walked us outside. I strapped Arianna in her car seat and gave Nina a kiss on the cheek. "Can I get one too?"

"Boy bye!" I said with a laugh. "You can get a hug."

"Dats gon' work."

I leaned in and gave him a hug. He held me close as my nostrils filled with the scent I had grown to love. I wished I could stay in his arms forever, but I knew it would take a miracle for that to happen. His hand grazed against my butt as he squeezed it in his hands. I pulled out of his arms, feeling goosebumps he had left behind on my entire body. I didn't know why I still felt so strongly for him. We had been broken up for well over a year, almost two years to be exact. Yet, I still held a special place in my heart for Dom. They say that happened when you found your first true love.

I guess he was mine…

Chapter four

Tory

After hanging with Dom today, I knew that dude wasn't ready for marriage. Hell, the fact that he was able to remain faithful to April all this time was a miracle in itself. Getting him down the aisle would take a lot more than a miracle. I wasn't saying he didn't love her. I just didn't think he understood exactly what he was getting into when he proposed. I mean, he already had a lot of responsibilities with eight kids. I think he thought that getting engaged would get him the pussy, and he was right. But, as far as I understood, she had given him the pussy already. He didn't need to propose to her.

The more I thought about it, the more I realized that wedding day was going to be a disaster. And lucky me, I was playing a major part as his best man. My job was to make sure that he made it down the aisle. But since I didn't think he was ready, I was going to talk him out of it. There was no need for him to do something he would regret later on, and I knew he would.

The chick Shawna who said she had a kid with him… well, that was another story. I wondered how he was going to break that news to April. I figured he wouldn't tell her about it though because he claimed the little boy wasn't his. However, he was basing that assumption on the color of the child's skin. If he would have taken a good look at that picture, he would have seen that the little boy had his nose and eyes. He looked like a lighter version of D.J. I suspected when Dom found out that really was his kid, he was going to have a major meltdown. I mean, who wouldn't in his shoes. After all, he already had eight, that we knew of. Who knew how many he really had out there?

I was headed home, but decided to make a stop first. My dick was hard and I needed some pussy to take the edge off. I pulled up to Krystal's apartment complex and parked my ride. I hopped out and headed up the stairs.

KNOCK! KNOCK! KNOCK!

She came to the door a couple of minutes later. "What are you doing here, Tory?"

She didn't look too happy to see me. Probably because we had an argument a couple of weeks ago about me leaving Ashley. Krystal claimed that she was tired of waiting for me to leave Ashley. She said she was tired of being faithful and loyal to a nigga who didn't share the same feelings. I cared about Krystal, a lot. I mean, she and I had been in this fuckship for over two years, three really. Of course, I had feelings for her. Sometimes, I even thought I might love her.

I pushed her inside as I shut the door. "I missed you," I said as I tried to kiss her. She turned her head so my lips landed on her cheek. "So, you don't miss me?"

"I'm tired, Tory. I'm tired of this half ass relationship. I'm tired of giving myself to you, so you can run back to that lil white bitch!" she said. I could see this was going to be harder than I thought. I needed Krystal right now. She was the only one that hadn't cheated on me. She hadn't fucked my best friend.

"I know, and I'm sorry. I'm just trying to make da right decision for my son," I said as I unbuttoned the button on her shorts.

She grabbed my hand before I could slide them off her hips. "How long do you expect me to just wait, huh?" She had a lone tear that ran down her cheek. I brushed it away with my thumb. I didn't want to hurt her feelings. She was a good girl and she didn't deserve that, but like I said, I had to make the best decision for my son.

"Not much longer…"

"I heard dat before," she sniffled.

"I mean it this time," I said as I brought my lips down to hers. She finally opened her mouth to receive my tongue.

As the kiss grew more passionate, I slipped her shorts off her hips. They crashed to the floor. I brought my fingers to her juice box and found that she wasn't even wearing panties. I slipped my fingers inside her as she moaned against my lips. As I worked my fingers inside her mushy center, I felt her gooey cream dripping. I scooped her up and carried her to the bedroom. We continued to kiss as I took long strides to get there.

Once inside the bedroom, I began to remove my clothes. She took her shirt off, revealing her perky C cup breasts. I climbed in the bed with her and got between her legs. I drove my tongue deep inside her pussy as she grinded into my mouth. Her pussy smelled so good, like fresh picked peaches or some shit like that. Her shit was definitely fruity. I began to tongue kiss her pussy as she went wild, screaming my name and everything.

Once I felt her cream in my mouth again, I slid my tongue out and climbed on top of her. As we kissed hungrily, I drove my dick inside her. Her pussy felt so good as it clung to my dick. She squeezed her pussy muscles around my dick, making my eyes cross and toes curl. I went deeper inside her as she held onto me. The passion I was experiencing with Krystal in that moment was something I had never felt with another chick before, not even Ashley.

I didn't even wanna fuck her at that moment. What I wanted was to make love to her. As I slowed the pace, I began to slowly grind my hips into her pelvis. She moaned as she held me close. I licked the right side of her neck, softly sucking on it. As she threw her pussy at me, I began to suck a little harder on her neck. That was the first time I had gone that far. I didn't know what was happening to me right now. I felt like a different person than I did when I first arrived.

As I lifted her legs in the crooks of my arms, all I wanted was to go deeper. For the next couple of hours, that was exactly what I did. I stayed in that pussy until I couldn't hold out any longer. I busted up inside her before collapsing next to her on the bed. As we struggled to catch our breaths, she slid into my arms. I held her close as she turned my head towards her.

"I love you, Tory. I've been loving you and after what happened just now, I think it's time for you to admit that you love me too," she said.

I stared at her in confusion. I knew she was right and that I did love her. I wasn't ready to admit it to her yet though. Holding back my feelings was what was keeping her in check. If I told her how I really felt, that shit would open up a whole can of worms that I wasn't ready for. I brought her head to mine and kissed her, long and deep. By the time I released her, I couldn't do shit but close my eyes. Sleep took over my body like you wouldn't believe. I guess it had to do with the alcohol and that good pussy.

Krystal

My name was Krystal, the other woman in Tory's life. I was aware that he was with that bitch, Ashley when we got together, but I couldn't help myself. I knew from the moment I met him that we'd be in a relationship. I just didn't think it would take this long for him to leave that bitch. I wasn't calling her a bitch because I was bitter from sleeping with Tory. I wasn't that petty. Well, yes I was, but not in that sense.

She was a bitch because she slept with his best friend, Dominic. I heard about that shit, not from him either. Everyone knew she had twins with two different daddies. You would have thought that would've been enough to make him leave her, but it wasn't. He was still there two years later and my patience was wearing really thin. I loved that man. I had been in love with him. I just didn't understand why it was taking him so long to leave that bitch.

I knew they had a son together. He said he didn't want to be apart from his son. I got that, but why couldn't he get custody of his little boy? Why couldn't he move in with me and we could raise him together? Why? Why? Why?

As he softly snored next to me, I slid out of the bed. I dug in his pocket for his phone, but the shit had a lock code on it. Dammit! It was cool though. I knew if I kept him sleeping here all night, eventually, his bitch would call. So, I had no intentions on letting him leave here tonight. I slipped his phone back in his pocked and climbed in bed beside him. I snuggled up close to him and kissed him softly on the lips. As he slept, I waited for that bitch to call.

*****

I must have dozed off because I was awakened by the buzzing of his phone vibrating. He was still sound asleep, so I slipped out of bed, hoping the phone would keep ringing. By the time I reached it, it had stopped. I crept into the front room and out the door as it began to vibrate again. I smiled when I saw her name on the screen. I couldn't wait to slide the phone to talk.

"Hello," I answered.

"Hello, I'm sorry. I must've dialed the wrong number," she said.

"Are you looking for Tory?"

"Yes…"

"Then you definitely dialed the right number," I said.

"Who is this and where's Tory? Is this the hospital? Has something happened to Tory?" she asked as she started to panic.

"No, this isn't the hospital and Tory is just fine. He's asleep actually," I said with a smile.

"Who is this? Put him on the phone now!"

"Bitch, don't you tell me what to do!" I growled.

"Bitch?"

"That's right, BITCH! Or would you prefer hoe, slut, thot? I mean, what else would I call you after you slept with Tory's best friend and had a baby by him? You're a fuckin' joke and you should know that Tory loves me. He doesn't love you anymore. He's only with you so he can be with his child," I said.

I could hear her crying on the other end of the phone, but I didn't give a shit. It seemed as if the only way I was going to get my man was to tell that bitch about us. Now that she knew, he would be free. "Now that you know about us, you can set him free. He doesn't love you anymore," I repeated.

"For your information, I known about your triflin' ass for a while…"

"Triflin'?"

"Yea, what else would you call someone who sleeps with a man who is already in a relationship? What else would I call you when you know we're engaged, but you still open your legs to him? You ain't nothin' but a triflin' side bitch! You'll never have him because he does love me and we have a family together," she said.

"That ain't his family. He has a son witcho hoe ass! That don't make y'all family," I said.

"Well, whether I have one, two or three kids by him, it's still more than you have. And it's enough to keep him. So, go have your little fun with him. But guess what? When you're done, he's going to put his clothes back on, walk out that door and come home to me," she said before she hung up. I was so mad, I wanted to scream. But, of course, seeing as how it was the middle of the night, I couldn't do that.

I walked back in the apartment, locked the door and headed to the bedroom. I slipped Tory's phone back in his pocket and climbed back next to him. I hoped he couldn't feel the chill from my body since I was standing outside butt ass naked. I turned my back towards his, purposely rubbing my ass against his dick. Sure enough, it sprung to life. I turned around and kissed my way down his stomach until I reached his magic stick.

I slid my tongue up and down his shaft before wrapping my lips around it. I began to slide my mouth up and down, rolling my tongue in a circular motion as I sucked. He moaned softly as I applied pressure to his dick with my mouth. Soon, he was thrusting his dick into my mouth. I didn't mind because I needed it to be as wet as possible before I slid my pussy on it. Tonight was the night I was going to get pregnant.

I removed my mouth from his dick and straddled him, sliding onto his slippery pole. It didn't take him long to grip my hips and start sucking on my breasts. I moaned softly as he circled my areola with his tongue. "Mmmmm!" I said as I rode his dick like a cowgirl in the Houston Rodeo.

"Aw shit!" he cried as I continued to pounce on that rod.

"You love this pussy, baby?" I asked.

"Fuckin' right!" he said as he plowed into me.

I felt my body shaking as I released my sugary goodness on his dick. He brought my head down and planted his mouth on mine. He stuck his tongue in my mouth, kissing me hungrily as I continued to ride his meaty stick. "Lemme hit it from the back," he said.

He didn't have to tell me twice. I jumped off his dick and dropped down on all fours, face down, ass up, just the way he liked to fuck. I spread my cheeks as he slid his tongue along the crevices of my wet pussy. "Oh, please put it in," I begged.

He slurped my juices before ramming his hard shaft into my pussy cat. "Sssshhhit!" I cried out as he plowed into me.

Our bodies slapped together in a sweaty, slippery mess as we gave each other what we needed in that moment. I loved Tory and if I couldn't get him from being loyal and faithful, I'd get him another way. I knew that he loved me, but was afraid to admit it. That was okay because I didn't mind taking the reins on this one. As he smashed my kitty from behind, I voiced my feelings for him.

"I love you, Tory. I love you so much," I said.

He reached for my face and kissed me as he continued to dip deep inside me. He released my mouth and began to punish my pussy. I cried out as he filled me with that dick I had grown to love over the years. I loved this man and one way or the other, I was going to have him. I deserved to be with him, not that cheating bitch he was with. I deserved his love, not her. If I had anything to say about it, I'd be announcing my pregnancy in a few weeks.

"Fuck me, baby!" I cried, which he was more than happy to do. He picked up the pace and began to bang my pussy out like he was trying to kill it. That was okay though. I figured the reason he was still coming to me was because the white girl couldn't handle his dick. White women liked small dicks, so sometimes, when they got a big black dick, they couldn't handle it.

I was definitely going to handle that dick for the rest of the night. Then, before he left in the morning, I'd handle that shit again. There wasn't nothing I wouldn't do for this man. That bitch thought she had one up on me, but I'd be damn.

I was sick and tired of waiting for him to make the decision to leave her. I understood he didn't wanna be apart from his child, but damn, I lived right around the corner from them. It wasn't like he couldn't pop over there on the daily and visit with or pick up his little boy. That bitch had me fucked all the way up if she thought I was just going to bow down and let her have him. If I had my way, he would've never gone back to her after he found out that one of those babies wasn't his.

He had cried on my shoulder, which I didn't mind because he gave me some dick afterward. That made me and him feel good. When he said he was going back to her, of course, I was hurt. But, when he explained that it was because he loved his son, I tried my best to be understanding. But a bitch like me could only be understanding for so long.

In the near distance, I heard his phone vibrating, so my moans turned to screams as I begged for him to fuck me harder. As he drove his dick deeper into my pussy while smacking my ass, I knew all thoughts of that bitch were out of his mind.

When we were done, once again, we cuddled and I rocked that ass to sleep. The last thought I had before I closed my eyes was I wondered if that bitch slept. As I was closing my eyes, his phone was still vibrating in his pants pocket, but he was already knocked out. I had one more ride before I sent him home to her. Shit, when I'd be done with him, there wouldn't be an ounce of energy left for her ass. I smiled at that thought, knowing that for the first time, I had the upper hand.

Chapter five

Tisha

Two weeks later...

Things between Reggie and I had been a little tense over the last few weeks. Sure, we talked and stuff, but it wasn't like before. I felt the only way I'd be able to get us back to a good place would be to have a baby by him. However, I didn't want another baby right now. So, was I supposed to compromise myself to please someone else? I loved Reggie with everything in me, but I just wasn't ready for another kid. For him to not understand how I felt was causing me to resent him. As much as I loved him, I didn't know if we could continue this way. While my kids were over at my mom's place for the afternoon, I decided now was as good a time as any to have a conversation with him.

He was sitting on the sofa watching college basketball when I sat next to him. For a few minutes, I sat quietly while I wondered if it was a good idea to even have this conversation. I didn't want to argue with him and I didn't want to break up either. But I didn't see how we could move on with so much tension between us.

"S'up?" he asked as he kept his gaze on the television screen.

"Can we talk?"

"Yea, sure," he said as he powered off the TV.

He turned to face me and waited for me to speak. I knew what I wanted to say, but I didn't know how to start it off. "Just say whatever's on your mind. You don't need to hesitate or think of what to say. Just spit it out," he said.

That was one of the reasons I loved him. No matter what, he always welcomed whatever I had to say. He knew me so well.

"Well, I wanna talk about the elephant in the room," I said.

He looked around the room and asked, "Where is it? I didn't notice an elephant in here."

"I mean…"

"I know what you mean, babe. Just trying to lighten the mood, I guess."

"I just don't like the space we're in these days. It's so much tension between us and I don't like it. I love you and if you love me…"

"IF I love you? What do you mean IF? You've never had to question my love for you before," he said.

"I know, but…"

"But what? Just because we have a disagreement or something, you think I don't love you? Tisha, I know what you've been through and I'd never play with your heart or feelings. If I didn't love you, trust me, I'd chuck the deuces to you and be out. I mean, we ain't got nothing holding us together but our love for each other," he said.

A tear slipped from my right eye and several more followed from both eyes. He brushed my tears away as he stared at me with love in his eyes. "I love you, babe. I never once wanted to hurt your feelings or make you cry. Come here." He pulled me into his arms as I cried against his shoulder. I loved Reggie so much, more than I had ever loved Dominic. Maybe I should give him the baby that he wanted. I didn't want to lose him and if that would keep him, then maybe that was what I needed to do.

"I just don't wanna lose you."

"You're not gonna lose me."

"If I don't have a baby, I will. I know how much you want one…"

"Hold that thought. I'll be right back," he said as he kissed me.

He walked into the bedroom and I heard him shuffling around in there. I wondered what he was doing because if he came back with a packed bag, I was going to lose it. It took him about five minutes before he returned. He walked over to where I was sitting and sat next to me.

"Do you believe that I love you?" he asked.

"Yes."

"Do you love me?"

"Of course, I do."

"Do you believe me when I tell you that I won't leave you?" he asked as he gave me a piercing stare.

"I guess so," I said.

"You guess so? I need you to know it for certain. I need you to tell me that you believe me when I say that I'm not going to leave you," he said.

"I believe you won't leave me," I said. He slipped off the sofa and got down on one knee before me. "What are you doing, Reggie?"

"Well, I was planning to do this in a more romantic setting, but I need you to know how much I love you. Tisha, since I met you, I felt as if I found my long lost best friend. We click on so many levels. I've never had a woman in my life who I vibed with so well. I know that I've been feeling some kind of way about having my own kid with you, but that's something that I have to deal with. I totally understand why you don't want anymore babies right now. I get it, babe and I'm sorry for acting so stupid. Just know that I'm here forever, if you'll have me," he said as he produced a small blue velvet box. Tears were already streaming from my eyes, so I had to brush them away so I could see what was in that box.

He pulled the lid open and it was a beautiful diamond ring. Not one of those big, gawdy rings that the celebrities have, but it was a nice size and it was beautiful. He looked up at me and I could see the love in his eyes. "Tisha Castle, will you have me to be your man for the rest of our lives?"

"Oh yes!" I cried as I fell into his open arms. He fell back on the floor as I smothered his face with kisses. "I love you so much." We continued to kiss on the floor like teens in high school. He pulled the ring out of the box and slid it onto my trembling finger. It looked so good there and I never thought I would find this much happiness.

As we began to kiss again, it became more passionate. This wasn't my boyfriend anymore. Reggie was now my fiancée and I couldn't wait to share my news with everyone. Reggie flipped me onto my back and penetrated me. Hell, I didn't even know how we got our clothes off. That was how much we were rolling on the floor. As I screamed in pleasure, he drove his dick in and out of me. I could feel my toes curling as my insides began to react from the orgasm that was building up.

"Oooohhhh shit!" I cried as it reached the surface.

I held him tighter as we began to kiss like we were hungry for each other. I felt his body shudder as he howled like a wolf. He brought his lips back down to mine and drove his tongue into my mouth. I wrapped my arms around him and kissed him with all the love I had in me. By the time we released each other, I was totally breathless.

He lay beside me as I gazed at my beautiful diamond ring. "You like it?" he asked as he pulled me close.

"I love it and I love you," I said as I kissed him on the lips. "When did you get this?"

"A couple of weeks ago."

"When were you going to give it to me?"

"For Valentine's Day," he said as he chuckled.

"Damn! Four months from now, Reg? Really?!" I asked as I play punched him in the arm.

"You were going to let Christmas pass by and give it to me for V Day?"

"Yep. I already have your Christmas gift," he said.

"Can I have it?" I asked with a sly smile.

"I'll give you half of it," he said.

"How you gon' gimme half of a gift?"

"Like this," he said and inserted his dick back inside me. For the next few hours, that was all we did; made love on the living room floor.

Chapter six

Dominic

I had been offshore for the past couple of weeks. I still hadn't gotten used to being out here without Slim yet. That dude was one of my best friends. Since his death, I was trying to maintain and do what I promised by taking care of my kids. I just didn't think it would be this hard. I kept remembering the last time he and I were out here. He was so excited about marrying Peaches. He couldn't stop talking about making her his wife. At the time, all I did was roll my eyes at him for being so damn happy. I was even pretending I was asleep just so I wouldn't have to listen to him.

Now, I wished that I had listened. If I could turn back the hands of time, I would have done things so much differently. I wouldn't have pretended to be asleep. I would've sat on the side of that bed and listened to his happy ass tell me how he felt. Even though it was hard for me to be on the water without my best friend, I was still happy to be away from all my troubles back home.

What troubles did I have? Well, for one, I was getting married in about five months. That shit had to be one of the scariest things I had ever had to face. I knew that I loved April, but I didn't think that I could marry her. I kept trying to find a way to tell her, but never figured it out yet.

I had been neglecting my kids and shit. I had no excuse for that. April said she understood that I had kids, but often tripped if I went by Tisha, Rasheeda or Trina's house. Shit, she had every reason to be worried about when

I went to Trina's house. She and I would fall into bed often when I needed some nookie. However, now that me and April were engaged, Trina refused to give me any of that good cookie. That was the only reason I had been faithful to April all this time.

Last time I visited my mom and Rasheeda was there, she was looking fucking good. She had lost all that weight and her body was shaped fine as hell. I wondered what she looked like without any clothes on, especially while she was bouncing that ass on my dick. Sometimes, when I had thoughts like that, I knew I couldn't marry April. Other times, I felt that she was a good influence on me and I needed to marry her. I honestly didn't know what the fuck I wanted.

What I did know was that I had promised myself after Slim died that I would be the dad that he was. He and Peaches had one little girl, but he treated her so good. I only wanted to treat my children the way they treated their daughter. I visited Peaches' mama sometimes because I wanted to check on her and Chrissy. I promised her that I'd do that from time to time. Plus, I wanted to make sure that Chrissy was okay. That was a promise that I was keeping to Slim.

My phone beeped as I was getting ready for bed. I looked at it and it was a message from April.

April: Hey bae, I was just checking on you

Me: Hey, I'm good

April: I miss you

Me: Me too

April: Are you still having six groomsmen in the wedding?

Me: Yea

April: Since we're getting married in the spring, I decided to go with a honeysuckle color for my dresses

Me: U mean pink? We ain't gay!

April: It's not pink

Me: I'm looking at it n it's pink. U gotta pick another color

April: But I like that color

Me: But u ain't marrying yourself

April: Damn! All this behind the color scheme

Me: I'm not wearing pink!!

April: Fine... I'll change it

Me: Good. I'ma hit u up later. I was going to bed

April: Ok... I love you

Me: Love u too

I put my phone on the charger and my hands behind my head. She was tripping if she thought I was about to put on a pink tie and shit. She had me fucked up. Pink wasn't an ugly color, but straight men didn't wear pink. At least, not from where I was from. If I would have known that was what she wanted to talk about, I would've never responded to that text. That was the shit that I was talking about.

I was all the way in the middle of the Gulf of Mexico and she had me pissed off about some pink shit. Why couldn't she just wait until I got back home? Next, I bet she come back with some bullshit color like periwinkle or something. That's the shit that bitches did though. Got under a nigga's skin behind some bullshit.

Chapter seven

Tory

Things between Ashley and I had been real tense since I came home that morning after being with Krystal all night. Since that night, she had been glaring at me with her evil eyes and shit. Did I care? Hell no! As far as I was concerned, this relationship had been over ever since she slept with Dom. She knew that nigga was my best friend and yet, she still seduced him with her booty shorts and tank top. What bitch would do that when she was supposed to love a man?

That morning I came in, she questioned me about my whereabouts. Of course, I lied to her because where I was shouldn't have been any of her business. I mean, was she honest with me when I asked her who was at our house that night? I mean, I specifically asked her if someone had dropped by and she said no.

"Where were you all night?" she asked.

She looked as if she hadn't slept a wink the whole night. I hoped she wasn't up worried about me because I was good. "Out," I responded.

Krystal had really worn me out, so all I wanted to do was take a shower and get in bed. I was glad that I was off today because that meant I could catch up on some sleep. Ashley had to work later though, but that was her business.

"Out where?"

"Why do I need ta tell you where I was? Out should be good enough."

"Out don't tell me nothin'!"

"I was just out, aight?"

"You were with dat bitch, weren't you?" she asked.

"I was just out," I replied.

"No, you were with her. I know you were."

"Whatever. I'm going take a shower and a nap before you go ta work."

I walked to the bedroom and she followed. "So, you think you're just gonna walk away and I'll stop talking?"

"I just wanna wash ma ass, ya feel me?"

"Yea, you wanna wash dat bitch's stank off yo ass, huh?" she asked.

"Look Ashley, I been out all night. It's 10 o'clock and I just wanna shower and take a nap before you go ta work. We can talk about dis shit lata," I said, hoping that would be the end of this conversation.

"I know you were with her because she answered your phone when I called you. You heard me, dat bitch told me you were with her when I called your phone. Do you know how dat made me feel? We're together and you were with dat other bitch last night, all night! What do you take me for, Tory? You think I ain't gon' leave you for treating me like shit?" she asked.

"Look Ashley, did you think about me when you was fuckin' ma boy, huh?" Her face immediately took on a look of hurt and pain. She didn't think I was gonna talk about it because I had been silent about it for about five months. I was honestly trying to make this relationship work with her,

but I didn't know how I could keep pretending to be happy with her.

"You said you forgave me for dat!" she said as tears streamed down her face.

"Forgiving you don't make it forgotten. We had a good relationship and you threw it away. You did dat!" I said.

"I said I was sorry!"

"And I'm supposed to be okay with it because you said sorry?"

"I know it's not ever gonna be da same again, but I was hoping..."

"You was hoping what? Dat I would say I forgive you and just forget? I can't forget! We was good, we was in a good place!" I said.

"No, we weren't. You been fuckin' dat bitch!" she said.

"So what? You coulda cheated on me with anybody else... with any other nigga! But you didn't! You chose ta cheat on me with ma best friend! Not only dat, but you got pregnant by him too! You got people laughin' at me and shit! Callin' me a sucka fa stayin' witcho ass! How you think dat shit make me feel, huh?" I asked her.

"I'm sorry. I've apologized a million times, but I can't change anything. I can't change what done already happened! How long you gon' keep punishing me?" she asked.

"You think I'm punishing you?"

"Well, why else would you be still sleeping with dat bitch?" she asked. As she looked at me, I could see something come across her face. I didn't know what it was. "You love her, don't you?" She waited for me to say something, but I couldn't. "Oh my God! You love her!" Now, she was in full blown crying mode. She was sniffling and hiccupping and I couldn't do shit about it. She was right. I did fall in love with Krystal. I knew that shit for a while now, but I wasn't going to admit it to anybody.

"I didn't say dat," I finally spoke up.

"You didn't have ta say it. It's written all over your face," she said.

I didn't know she could read my face like that. I hadn't even told Krystal that I loved her yet, but Ashley had figured it out.

"What now? Are you leaving me for her?" she asked as she continued to sob.

"I didn't say dat."

"So, you're in love with another woman and you expect me ta just be okay with dat?"

"I don't know how I expect you ta feel about it. I guess you can feel about it da same way I felt when I found out dat Kyon wasn't mine. You remember me askin' you if you had fucked another nigga? You remember me askin' you if dat baby could be fa somebody else, huh? Did you tell me da truth?" I asked. "Hell naw! You just kept lyin' ta me and shit!"

"I'm sorry. I'M SORRY!" she yelled, causing the boys to start crying. "You need ta make a decision because I ain't finna be no side bitch."

"Side bitch?! How you da side bitch when we live together?" I asked.

"Then I guess I'm da main bitch, but either way, I ain't finna play second fiddle to no other bitch! If you can't stop cheating on me because you love her, then you need ta go be with her. As much as dat shit would break my heart because I really love you, I'ma just have ta let you go," she said as she dried her eyes and left the room. A short time later, I heard her trying to soothe the twins.

I grabbed my phone and sent Krystal a text message.

Me: That wasn't cool what you did

Krystal: What did I do?

Me: You know exactly what you did. You answered my phone when Ashley called

Krystal: She don't deserve you

Me: That's all you gotta say?

Krystal: I love you

Me: That wasn't cool

I walked into the bathroom and turned on the shower.

Now, she was looking at me all crazy while the kids played with their toys. We had barely said two words to each other since the argument we had. I didn't know what was gonna become of this relationship. I didn't want to be apart from my son. He was the most important person in my life. I didn't know how things would work out if we separated. My little boy was used to seeing me every day. I knew it would stress him out if all of a sudden, I wasn't there anymore. That was the shit I struggled with the most.

My son was more important to me than anyone else in this world. The last thing I wanted was for him to whine and cry for me and I wasn't there. We, as parents, were supposed to put our wants aside for the sake of our children. That was what I was doing. Even though I loved Krystal, I was putting aside my happiness for my son. I just didn't know how long I could continue depriving myself of the happiness that I deserved.

"You gon' keep lookin' at me crazy or you gon' say somethin'?" I asked.

"What da hell you want me ta say dat I ain't already said?"

"I'on know. I just want you ta stop lookin' at me with dat weird look on yo face."

"Oh, so my face is weird na?"

"I guess it is," I said.

"Whatever Tory. If you don't wanna be with me, then don't. I love you, but I'm tired of begging you ta forgive me. Dat shit dat happened between me and Dom ain't never gonna change, so I'on know whatchu want me ta say," she said.

"I ain't ask you ta say shit! Say whatever you wanna say!"

"I ain't got nothin' else ta say. Do whatever you wanna do!"

I just shook my head. She didn't have to tell me that shit because I was already doing what I wanted to do. I just didn't know if I'd be able to stay with Ashley when my heart wasn't in it. I loved my son more than anything and for that reason alone, I was still living here. I'd always care about Ashley because she was the mother of my son. I just didn't know if I'd ever be able to sacrifice my happiness to remain with her. But wasn't a parent supposed to do what was best for their child, regardless of whether they were happy about the situation or not?

That was what gave me conflicted emotions. I didn't want to seem as though I didn't care about my son's needs or that I was putting my needs before his. I just didn't know if it was doing anyone any good to have me and Ashley stay together. I knew eventually, she'd begin to hate me for not loving her the way she deserved. And I'd begin to resent her for having stayed with her. This would be a hard decision for me to make, so I had to make sure I made the right one.

Chapter eight

Krystal

Two months later…

I sat down in the bathroom waiting for the results of the Clear Blue Easy Pregnancy Test. Even though I already knew what the results were, I still wanted to take the test to show Tory. I had planned that shit so perfectly. I knew once I told him that I was pregnant, he would leave that bitch to be with me. This wasn't my first time getting pregnant by Tory. But this would be the first one he knew about though. This was actually my third pregnancy by him, which was why I knew that I was indeed pregnant.

I aborted the first pregnancy because we had just started messing around and I didn't want him to feel trapped by me. Not only that, but I was younger at the time and I wasn't ready to be a mommy. I had just started college and had a part time job, so I wasn't making the money that was necessary to take care of anyone but myself. When I found out that I was pregnant the second time, I wouldn't say that I was overjoyed or anything like that, but I wasn't unsure like the first time. The second time, I was in my junior year of college, but I was doing clinicals and had a better job. I knew that I'd be able to take care of my baby that time.

But I guess God felt I wasn't ready since I had a miscarriage during my third month. I wasn't devastated by the loss of my baby, but I was a little hurt. I hadn't even told Tory about the baby yet, nor did he know anything about the first one. When I lost the second baby, I just thanked God for taking it from me sooner, rather than later.

At least, I hadn't had time to bond with the little one yet. I couldn't imagine the pain I would've felt had I been further along when I lost the baby.

I watched as the big plus sign appeared in the little window, revealing what I already knew. I was pregnant with Tory's baby and if God said the same, this one would make it to term. I was going to do everything right so that my baby could enter the world healthy. I smiled as I thought about sharing the news with Tory. I had sent him a text, knowing he was at work. I was just waiting for him to hit me back.

I just needed him to come by when he got off work. I knew it was going to be late though because he didn't get off until one o'clock in the morning. Aside from that, it took him an hour to get back to this side of town. That was alright with me though. I didn't mind waiting up for him. Hell, I'd even make him something to eat. I needed to tell him our good news about our baby. I just hoped that he would give me the reaction that I wanted.

My phone beeped, letting me know that a text message had come through. I picked up my phone and got all giddy when I realized that it was Tory. Believe it or not, he was the only man that made my heart dance that way. Ever since the day we met three years ago, my heart had beat the same way just for him.

Tory: I'm really tired, babe. Can this wait?

I had to look twice at that message because I couldn't believe he was trying to blow me off. What the hell kind of voodoo, cush cush, kinda shit was that? He was never too tired to drop by before. What the hell was that bitch doing to him over there?

Me: No, babe… it can't wait. I really need to see you

Tory: Okay, I'll come by, but I can't stay over. That girl was really trippin' last time

Me: I don't give two snap beans of a fuck if she was trippin'!

Tory: I'll text you when I'm on my way

Me: Okay… I love you

Tory: C u when I get there

I let it go like that, but I wasn't happy. Deep down in his heart, I knew he loved me. I often wondered why he kept holding back on letting me know. Maybe it was because of that bitch and the hold she had on him or maybe, it had to do with his little boy as always. I knew one thing though… if it had to do with that bitch, it wouldn't have shit to do with her when I was done tonight.

I busied myself for the rest of the evening, even taking a shower and a nap.

*****

At 1:30 in the morning, my alarm on my phone rang. I quickly silenced the aggravating noise and slid out of bed. I had cooked earlier, so I made my way to the kitchen to make Tory a plate. I placed the plate in the microwave and waited until I heard his car pull up. I had given him a key over a year ago, so I just waited for him to let himself in. Once he entered the apartment, I stood in the doorway in his t-shirt and a pair of short boy shorts.

"Hey baby," I greeted him in my most sultry voice.

"Babe, I told you that I was tired. If you asked me over here just for sex…"

The timer beeped on the microwave, so I retreated to the kitchen. I grabbed his plate of food and a glass of ice cold Coke and headed back to the living room where he was waiting. I set the Coke down and handed him the plate of food. I had cooked his favorite; crawfish etouffee over rice with jalapeño hushpuppies and potato salad. He tore into the food while watching the sports highlights. I got up from the sofa and went into the bedroom to receive the pregnancy test. I returned to the living room to find him finishing the last of his food.

"Damn, that shit was off the chain! Thanks babe," he said as he grabbed the glass of Coke.

"You're welcome," I said as I flashed all my pearly whites.

Once he was finished drinking his Coke, he stood up. "Where are you going?" I asked.

"Home."

"Babe, I really needed ta talk ta you. I mean, I didn't invite you hear just ta eat."

"Oh, I'm sorry. Can you make it fast? I'm so fuckin' tired."

"Yea, sure. Close your eyes," I said.

"C'mon bae, you gon' fuck around and make ma ass fall asleep right here," he said.

"Just close your eyes please."

He did as I asked and shut his eyes. I put the test in front of his face, but not directly and said, "Okay, you can open them now."

He opened his eyes and set them on the test. As he stared at the positive sign, he looked over at me. I had on this smile that was bigger than a kid at Christmas. "Uh, you're pregnant?" he finally asked.

"Yep," I said as I jumped into his arms.

He hugged me back, but his stance was as stiff as a piece of plywood. I slowly pulled myself from his arms and studied his face. He didn't look happy, but he didn't look mad either. If I had to guess, I'd say he had an expression that reflected total shock.

"You're not happy?" I asked.

"I didn't say that. I'm just shocked, is all."

"Babe, I'm so excited and happy to be having your baby," I said.

"I can tell."

"Babe, we're having a baby. After three years, we're finally having a baby!" I said as I threw my arms around his neck. I didn't feel that he was too happy, so I decided to try a different approach. I pulled out of his arms again and took his hands. I placed his right hand on my belly and said, "Can you believe it? We have a little baby growing in here. Like, a little bun in the oven."

He gently rubbed my belly as tears sprang to his eyes. "Aw baby, I didn't mean to make you cry," I said as I wiped his tears and kissed him gently on the lips. I didn't think he'd be that emotional. I wrapped my arms around his neck and this time he held me tight. "We can be a family, babe. I love you so much."

I was standing on my tiptoes as he held me. I moved my face to the left and touched his lips with mine. I wrapped my arms tightly around his neck as the kiss grew heated. He lifted me up and carried me to the bedroom. So far, I was very pleased with how things were going. As he laid me on the bed, I waited for him to take off his clothes. Instead, his face took on a blank stare as he looked down at me.

"What's wrong, baby?" I asked.

"You're pregnant," he said as he slumped down at the foot of my bed.

I wasn't ready for our heated session that had just started to end. I stood up from the bed and made my way to the bathroom. I turned the water on and then walked back into the bedroom to find Tory still sitting in the same spot with his face in the palm of his hands. I could tell that he was a little stressed out. I grabbed his hand and pulled him from the bed. He allowed me to lead him into the bathroom. I began to undress him and when he was butt naked, I removed my clothes and led him into the shower. As he stood there, looking all sexy and handsome, with the water falling all over him.

I really loved that man with all my heart. The fact that we had created a little one would only bring us closer. As I lathered him with soap, he leaned his head back, allowing the water to trickle down over the two of us. When I was done soaping him up, he stood underneath the warm spray to rinse it off. Then I wrapped my arms around his neck as I moved closer to him. We began to kiss each other hungrily and I could feel his dick growing against me.

It didn't take long for him to scoop me up in his arms, inserting his hard member inside me. I gasped as he hit my special spot, causing me to cream immediately. As he gripped my butt cheeks in his strong hands, he worked my kitty up and down on his pole. I held on to him as we moaned deeply. The feel of this man inside me was amazing.

BANG! BANG! BANG!

The noise on my front door caused us to both look at each other. I didn't know who the hell was at my door at three in the morning, but I damn sure wasn't going to answer it. We continued to make love as the water sprayed both of our hot bodies.

BANG! BANG! BANG!

"Who the fuck is dat?" he asked as he placed my feet on the shower stall floor.

"I don't know!" I said and I was dead serious.

He turned the water off and stepped out, grabbing a towel from the countertop next to the shower. He wrapped it around him and I did the same with my towel. I knew he probably thought that I was lying when I said I didn't know who was at my door, but I really didn't. I had never stepped out on or cheated on Tory the whole time we've been together. Why the hell would I start now?

BANG! BANG! BANG! BANG!

He rushed to the front room and pulled the door back.

"I KNEW YOU WERE OVER HERE WHEN YOU DIDN'T COME HOME!!" I was stunned for a minute. Why the fuck was this bitch on my doorstep? I had never gone to her house once, yet, there she stood, disrespecting my shit at three in the damn morning.

"What are you doing here, Ashley?" Tory asked the question I damn well needed the answer to.

She walked to her car and returned with two large black garbage bags. She dropped them on my doorstep and said, "Since this is where yo ass wanna be, you can stay here! As of now, WE ARE OVER!"

Shit, I couldn't have asked for more at that moment. "Thank you, bitch! I was wondering how long it was gon' take you ta let him go!" I said.

"Bitch?! BITCH?! YOU ARE FUCKIN' MA MAN AND YOU CALL ME A BITCH?! YOU GOT A LOTTA FUCKIN' NERVE, BITCH!" she yelled back.

This was not how I expected this night to go. I mean, she was about to have my neighbors calling the damn police. "Get the fuck off my doorstep!" I said.

"I can't believe you, Tory! After all we've been through! We have a son!" she cried. "We were a family!"

"Well, we're a family now," I said as I rubbed my belly.

The pained expression on her face was very clear. I knew Tory probably didn't want that part brought out tonight, but I had to say something. That bitch had given him to me and I was going to make sure she never took him back. She didn't even bother to answer as she shook her head, got in her car, and backed out of the parking spot. He picked up the bags and brought them in my apartment.

"Now what did you do dat for?" he asked.

Aw shit! I knew I had done too much, but hell, he knew I was extra when he started fucking with me. He shouldn't have been surprised by how far I'd go to keep him. I loved him.

Chapter nine

Tory

The last thing I expected when I dropped by Krystal's place was to stay over. I had just come over because she said she had something important to speak to me about. When I got here and she had cooked my favorite food. She knew how much I loved crawfish etouffee. Not only that, but she told me she was pregnant. More than anything, I wanted to run up outta there, but I wasn't raised that way. I was a man and I knew that was my baby, so if she was pregnant, I owed it to her to be here for her. After all, she was the one I loved.

I hated that I'd have to hurt Ashley, but after everything we had been through, I knew she saw this shit coming. I hadn't had the chance to even process Krystal's news when she dragged me into the bathroom and began undressing me. I allowed her to do that because I was tired. I had worked ten hours tonight and I was exhausted.

I had no idea that shit was going to come to a blow tonight though. Krystal and I were in the shower making love when we heard that banging on the front door. I didn't know who the fuck that was, but if it was a nigga, I was gonna kick both their asses. If Krystal had been cheating on me, I knew I didn't have a right to be mad, but gotdammit, I was gonna hurt somebody.

I jumped out of that shower and rushed to the front door. I just knew that was a nigga at that door and so help me God if it was. Had I known what was waiting for me on the other side, I never would've answered. I pulled the door back ready to bust a nigga in his chops. But instead of a nigga, Ashley stood there with tears in her eyes. I had no idea what the fuck she was doing here. I mean, it was after three in the damn morning.

The only question that I could think of to ask was what she was doing here. The rage mixed with hurt on her face had me feeling sick to my stomach. On one hand, she shouldn't have been that hurt considering everything she had put me through. On the other hand, I understood why she was pissed. If it had been me that had caught her ass at another nigga's place, I would've had to fuck somebody up.

I had no idea that Krystal was going to reveal that she was pregnant tonight. She had just told me the news and I was still processing it. I was still trying to figure out what to do. But with Ashley dumping my clothes and shit on Krystal's doorstep like that, I already knew I wasn't going back there. I wasn't expecting Ashley to be so hurt though. Number one, she already knew about Krystal. Number two, she said she knew that I didn't love her anymore. Number three, she had hurt me so much. Did she really think I was going to just be able to get past that shit?

I tried, God knew I tried, to get over the fact that she had slept with my best friend. I thought I had gotten over it, but I hadn't. I should've ended things with Ashley as soon as I found out that Kyon wasn't mine. But I didn't want Keenan to feel some kind of way about not seeing me every day. I loved my son so much that I was willing to stay with Ashley even if I was miserable. But the shit had finally hit the fan and she had thrown me out. It was cool though. I shouldn't have been there that long in the first place.

"Why are you looking at me like dat?" Krystal asked.

"Why would you tell her dat shit tonight? I mean, I just found out. Couldn't you have left well enough alone? She had already thrown all ma shit out!" I said.

"Well, I just thought dat she should know you didn't need her ass. You really don't need her, baby. I'm da one who really loves you," she said as she walked closer to me.

I didn't want to become distracted by her coming on to me, but I was still horny. I allowed her to approach me. When she got closer to me, she pulled at my towel and it fell to the floor. As she stroked my manhood, we kissed. As the fire began to burn inside me, all thoughts of Ashley were out the window. I opened Krystal's towel and scooped her up. As I pushed my hard dick inside her, she held on to my neck.

"Mmmm!" she moaned in my ear.

"Fuck!" I cried as I pummeled inside her.

"I love you, Tory," she cried.

"I love you too," I finally admitted. I mean, as long as things with me and Ashley were over, I could tell Krystal exactly how I felt about her. It seemed like after I spoke those four words, her bounce on my dick became fiercer. I walked her to the bedroom and placed her sexy body on the bed. As she opened her legs wider, I plowed deep inside her, grinding my hips slowly.

"Oh God!" she cried. "Mmmm!"

Being inside Krystal's pregnant pussy right now had me feeling good as hell. I loved pregnant pussy because for some reason it felt better than regular pussy. I wondered why that was. I wondered why when a woman was pregnant, her kitty felt better than ever. I wished that Krystal could stay pregnant forever, just so I could lay in it.

Once we were done satisfying our cravings, we laid in bed together. "So, what now?" she asked.

"It's up ta you. I mean, we can either live together and become a family, or I can get ma own place."

"You serious right now? I've been wanting you here wit me."

"I'm just saying, ya know?"

"Well, I like the first option. I love you, Tory and I wanna be wit you and no one else."

"I love you too."

"You don't know how happy I am ta finally hear you admit dat ta me."

"Yea, I know. It's not dat I didn't wanna tell you. It's just dat it felt wrong ta tell you dat I love you when I was still living with her. Now dat I'm living with you, I can tell you how I feel without feeling guilty," I said.

"Are you done wit her fa good?"

"Whatchu mean?"

"I mean, what if she asks you ta come back…"

"She won't. Even if she did, I wouldn't go back," I said.

"So, we're finally gonna be together? Like fa real, fa real?" she asked excitedly.

"Yea, like fa real, fa real."

It felt good to be lying in bed with Krystal. It felt good to have shit all out on the table, even if things didn't happen the way I wanted them to.

"Can I get some sleep now, bae? I'm exhausted," I said.

"Yea, I'm tired too. Can we cuddle?" she asked.

"Yea, just as long as you let me get some sleep."

So, as hard as it was for me to not get back in that pussy, I didn't. As I held Krystal and inhaled her sweet scent, I closed my eyes and fell asleep. The sun would be up soon enough and then I'd have to deal with Ashley again. I hoped that I wouldn't get any flack from her when it came time to visiting my son. Lord help her if she ever tried to keep me from my kid.

Chapter ten

Dominic

I had been offshore for the past four and a half months. I didn't usually take jobs as long as that anymore, but since I was taking two months off to get married... well, you knew how that shit went. I finally made it back to land and April was waiting for me. She rushed over to give me a hug and smother me with kisses in front of every fucking body. I knew she missed me, but damn. This was the reason I didn't like when she picked me up. As my co-workers all oohed and aahed like teenagers, I slowly pushed her off me and put my things in the car. As I got behind the wheel, she slid into the passenger's seat.

"Is something wrong?" she had the nerve to ask.

"Naw, I'm just tired," I lied because I didn't feel like arguing.

She pouted for a couple of minutes before she started speaking again. "So, I changed the color of the bridesmaids' dresses. Well, the colors of the whole wedding to be exact."

There she went, talking about the wedding again. I hadn't even been in the car with her for a good ten minutes. Instead of arguing, I decided to play along. "What colors did you decide on?"

"Okay, I thought the colors of the wedding could be silver, ivory and sunset," she said happily.

"What da hell is sunset?" I asked.

"It's like a rust orange color, but not as dark. Here, let me show you," she said as she opened up her phone. She looked through her phone for a couple of minutes, then turned it towards me. "See, the colors will be so pretty together. I saw them in a Vogue magazine."

"Vogue? That shit expensive as hell!"

"Yea babe, but we can afford it," she said with a huge smile.

We, she said. We, meaning she, had been dipping into my bank account for this wedding for the past three months. The first thing I did when I hit the dirt was log into my bank account. The amount she had spent while I was gone nearly knocked me off my fucking feet. Speaking of which…

"Can I have my debit card back please?" I asked as I held out my hand.

"What? Why?"

"I just need my shit back."

"But I still have a few more things I need to pay for," she retorted.

"Then YOU pay for it. You've been using all ma damn money ta pay for a wedding dat yo family supposed ta be helping wit! Look, I just got back, I'm tired as hell, so I ain't finna argue witchu. All I want is fa you ta put ma card in ma hand, so I can put da shit back in ma own damn pocket."

She opened up her expensive handbag, probably something she treated herself to with my money, and handed me my bank card. She sat on the other side of the car, pouting like a six-year old child. The rest of the ride home was quiet as hell, but I wasn't complaining. I didn't feel like hearing all that talk about the wedding anyway. I knew she wasn't about to give me no fucking pussy though, but it was cool. I had a few places to go anyway, once I showered and got dressed.

*****

I finally pulled into the driveway of our house and turned the ignition off. I slid out of the driver's seat and grabbed my bag out the trunk. She rushed inside because she was still pissed off. I made it inside, closed and locked the door. I went into the bedroom and headed straight for the walk-in closet. I dumped my bag on the floor and headed to the bathroom. I needed to take a shit before I jumped in the shower.

I locked the bathroom door and sat on the toilet. While I was sitting there, I sent a text to Trina.

Me: Hey girl, wyd

She took a few minutes to respond back…

Trina: At work… why?

Me: Cuz I'm home n wanted 2 come slide thru

Trina: No thanks

Me: Y not?

Trina: I'm done Dom… I'm not playing this game with you no more. You want to slide through something? Slide it in your fiancée. Don't text, call or pop up no more for this pussy b/c my shop is closed to you.

Me: Y u acting like that?

Trina: If it don't concern our daughter, don't contact me. Bye!

Well damn! Now what the fuck was I supposed to do? I decided to hit up Rasheeda. She had been calling me for weeks about something important she needed to tell me. I knew she still wanted me, so I was gonna see what she was talking about.

Me: Wassup

Rasheeda: Are you back home?

I knew she wanted some more of that wood. As fine as her thick ass had gotten, I'd be more than happy to give her some of this wood. I knew she missed me and this dick. We hadn't fucked in damn near three years. I knew that old dude wasn't hitting it right or they'd still be together. But I knew how to hit it though, and I knew that pussy was tight. Just thinking about how it would feel wrapped around my dick had it hard.

Me: Yea, wassup

Rasheeda: Have you gone by your mom's yet?

What the hell? What did my mom have to do with her giving me some pussy?

Me: Not yet. I just got back. Y?

Rasheeda: You should go see her. She hasn't been feeling well.

What the hell she mean my mom was sick? I know I hadn't spoken to her in a few weeks, but damn. What the hell could've happened to her in the little while that I hadn't spoken to her? I decided to call Rasheeda and find out what the heck she was talking about. Let me find out my mom had a cold or something and Rasheeda was blowing that shit out of proportion. Rasheeda's phone rang twice before she picked up.

"Hey Dom."

"Aye, how you doin'?"

"I'm good, a little tired, but good. How bout you?"

"I'm straight. Look, what's going on wit ma mom?" I asked.

"You haven't spoken to her?" she asked.

"Nah, I just got back I told you."

"Well, your mom's been going through it…"

"Whatchu mean going through it? She got the flu or somethin'?" I hoped that wasn't what she had because that fucking flu epidemic been killing people left and right.

"No, but she's really sick, Dom. Do you remember that day you came by to visit her when Ari and I were there? You remember how tired she was?"

"Yea, but what that got ta do wit her sickness? I had got her some vitamins and orange juice. Dat shit didn't help?"

I heard crying in the background and she said, "Y'all play nice if y'all want some ice cream later."

"Who all ova there?" I asked.

"Just me, Ari and Nina," she said.

"Nina? What the hell Nina doin' ova there?"

"I've had her for the past three weeks. I told you that your mom ain't been feeling good."

"Yea, but I didn't think it was dat serious," I said.

"It is. Dats why I asked had you been ta see her yet."

"How serious?"

"Just go see your mom, Dominic. I've been helping her the best I can, but it's been hard. That's why I'm glad you're back home," she said.

"What's wrong wit her?" I asked.

"I think you should just go see her. I'm here if you need me."

"Yea, aight."

I ended the call and wiped my ass. Why did Rasheeda make it seem like my mom was dying or something? I flushed the toilet and washed my hands. I dialed my mom's phone, but got no answer. I hit the 'send' button again to redial. After four rings, she finally picked up.

"Hello," some strange woman answered. I pulled the phone away from my ear to make sure I had dialed the right number. Yep, I sure had, so who the fuck had my mom's phone?

"Who da fuck is dat and whatchu doin' wit ma mom's phone?"

"Excuse you," she said.

"Nah nigga, excuse yo ass! Where da fuck ma mom at?" I barked into the phone.

"Oh wow! You must be Dominic. Ms. Belinda has told me so much about you," the woman said.

"Well, that's funny cuz she ain't told me a damn thang about you. Who da fuck are you and where ma mama at?"

"I thought we'd make the introductions in person..."

"Fuck all dat! If you don't tell me who da fuck you are and where ma mama at..."

"I'm trying to tell you, sir. My name is Jennifer and I'm a nurse that was hired to take care of your mother," she said.

"A nurse? Hired to take care of my mom? Where the fuck she at?"

I was about to lose my mind up in this bathroom with my dick swinging all over the damn place. What the fuck did my mom need a damn nurse for? None of that shit was making any sense.

"Sir, why don't you just come over to visit your mom? I know Ms. Belinda will be happy to see you and I can explain to you who I am in person," she suggested.

"Oh, you best believe I'm finna come over there!" I said as I ended the call.

I hopped in the shower real quick, anxious to get over to my mom's and find out what the hell was going on. I lathered myself up good before rinsing myself off. Then I stepped out and dried myself off. I walked into the bedroom and started getting dressed.

"Where are you going?" April asked.

"Ta check on ma mom."

"What's wrong with your mom?"

"You could be telling me dat had you gone ta see her while I was gone," I said.

"Oh, so now you have an attitude with me for not visiting your mom while you were gone. I had a lot to do, Dominic. Do you know how hard it is to plan a wedding?"

"You really think I give a shit about dat wedding right now! The only thing I'm worried about is ma mom!" I said.

When I was finished getting dressed, I grabbed my keys. "You want me to come with you?" she asked.

"Naw, you had four months ta check on her and you didn't!"

"I was busy planning…"

"I know… da wedding! I'm so sick of hearing about dat damn wedding!" I said as I mugged her.

I could see how hurt she was and I didn't mean to hurt her feelings, but right now, the last thing I cared about was getting married. I rushed out the door and jumped in my truck. I had upgraded my car to a 2017 GMC Denali a few months ago. I loved this truck. It was definitely made just for me.

*****

It took me half an hour to get to my mom's place because of the traffic. After I parked my truck, I hurried inside the house. I was met at the door by a tall, slim black beauty. "Hello," she said with a startled expression on her face.

"Who are you?" I asked.

"Are you Dominic?"

"Yea, so who are you?"

"Well, as I told you on the phone, I'm Jennifer, your mom's nurse."

"What does my mom need a nurse for?" I asked.

"Well, your mom is very sick," she said.

"Yea, so I heard. Where is she?"

"She's in the bedroom resting."

I turned on my heels and headed towards my mom's bedroom. Now, I knew that Jennifer and Rasheeda had said my mom was sick, but nothing prepared me to see her in the condition she was in. The woman lying in that bed wasn't the same woman I saw a few months ago. The woman in that bed was frail and weak. She had lost a lot of weight and her skin was so pale. I rushed over to her bedside and sat down.

"Mom," I said as I waited for her to open her eyes.

She opened them and turned to face me. "Hey baby," she said with a weak smile.

"Hey ma, what's going on? I mean, what happened ta you?"

"Aw baby, I'm just a little sick."

"A little? Be honest wit me, ma because you look more than a little sick," I said.

"Okay," she said as she started coughing. The second cough, blood flew from her mouth. Now, I was truly concerned. Jennifer rushed over and handed her some paper towel. She wiped her mouth and Jennifer handed her a cup of ice water with a straw in it. She took a couple of sips and Jennifer took the cup and set it on the table. That was when I noticed all the medication on the table.

I looked at my mom, then at Jennifer. What the hell was wrong with my mom? Why was she spitting up blood and taking all that medication? "Ma, clearly you're more than just a little sick. What's going on?"

"Can we talk about this later, baby? I'm so tired," she said.

"Aight, getchu some rest," I said and kissed her forehead. I didn't want to just leave it at that, but I didn't wanna push her when she was clearly exhausted. As she closed her eyes, I walked out of the room.

"She has cervical cancer," Jennifer said from behind me.

"What?!" I asked as I turned to face her.

"Your mom has cervical cancer."

"What do you mean? How serious is it?" I asked.

"Very serious, it's at stage four," she said.

"What's stage four?"

"Well, cancer has four stages and your mom has stage four B."

"What da hell is stage four B? I mean, what are you sayin'?" I asked.

"You want the truth?"

"Is my mom gonna die?"

"The cancer has spread to other parts of her body. The doctors are trying to remain hopeful for her sake, but they aren't sure if she'll make it through the year," she said with a sad expression on her face.

Tears immediately sprung to my eyes. Was this nurse telling me that my mom was dying? Oh my God! This wasn't what I wanted to hear after just getting back. I couldn't say shit. I just walked out the door. I didn't know what to do. I thought about calling Tory, but I needed to talk to someone who knew what my mom was going through. I headed to Rasheeda's place.

Chapter eleven

Rasheeda

I hadn't heard from Dom since he called me earlier.
I hoped that he had a chance to speak to his mom. I had
gone to her house yesterday to bring Nina for a visit, but
she was so weak, all she could do was sleep. Nina cried
every time I took her to visit her mom, but only when it
was time to leave. I was sure she hated being without her
mom. I mean, she was only one year old. Once we got to
the car, all her crying had stopped. I wanted to call Dom
and check on him, but I figured after hearing the news
about his mom, he probably wouldn't want to talk.

KNOCK! KNOCK! KNOCK!

I was sitting on the sofa with the girls watching the
Trolls movie for the umpteenth time. I walked over to the
door as the girls continued to watch TV. I pulled the door
open and there stood Dom, all handsome and smelling
good. One look at his face and I knew he had seen his
mom. I just took him by the hand and pulled him inside. As
soon as I closed the door, I wrapped my arms around him.
He started crying on my shoulder as soon as I did that. I
was shocked by his reaction because I had never seen him
cry before.

I was sure he had cried when his best friend, Slim
had died, but since I didn't attend the services, I didn't see
it. Now, seeing him this vulnerable and heartbroken made
me love him even more than I already did. The girls came
running over to us and wrapped their little arms around his
legs. Nina was crying, probably because she hadn't seen
her brother cry before. Ari wasn't crying though because

she was just happy to see her daddy. She hadn't seen him in almost six months and I knew she missed him. I knew she was excited to see him by the thrill in her voice.

He finally released me and dried his eyes. He leaned over and picked up the two little girls. They wrapped their arms around his neck and held him tight. He walked over to the sofa and sat with them on his lap. "Daddy, why you cry?" Arianna asked him.

It broke my heart to see him that way. All I wanted was to offer him some form of comfort, but I didn't know what to do. "Daddy's okay," Dom responded. "How my girls been doing?"

"Miss you, daddy," Ari said.

"Daddy missed you too. I missed you too, Nina."

He kissed them on the cheeks before I said, "Why don't you two girls go sit down in the big chair so I can talk to daddy."

They hopped off his lap and made their way to the big chair. "You okay?" I asked.

"Hell no, I'm not okay! I just found out dat my mom is dying," he said.

"I'm so sorry, Dom. I wanted to tell you, but I didn't think a text message was the way to deliver that kind of news," I said. I really felt for him right now. I didn't know what I'd do if it were me facing the loss of my mom. The thing that hurt the most was that there was nothing I could do to ease his pain or make it better.

"How long have you known?" he asked.

"Well, a couple of weeks after you left, she asked me to go with her to the doctor. She was still feeling really tired. I mean, she had no energy at all, no matter how much she rested. I agreed to go with her, mostly to watch the kids, but I was also worried about her. The doctor ran a bunch of tests and gave her a woman's exam. After running more tests, she finally called her back in and gave her the news."

"The nurse said it's bad and dat she got about six months," he said with tears in his eyes.

"That's because the cancer spread to the inside of her liver and other organs..."

"Whatchu mean other organs?" he asked.

"Well, because they weren't able to catch it sooner, it spread to her lungs. That's why the doctor said her time is limited."

"Well, can't they do some kind of treatment ta save her?"

"Not from what I understand. I'm so sorry," I said as I rubbed the back of his hand with my own.

"This just seems like a bad fuckin' dream, yo."

"I know. Look, it's getting kind of late. How about you help me feed the girls? Then, I'll give them a bath. Then you can help me put them to bed. That might make you feel better," I said.

His phone started ringing. He pulled it from his back pocket and swiped ignore. I caught a glimpse of who was calling before he ignored it and shoved the phone back in his pocket. I wondered why he didn't wanna talk to his fiancée. But I wasn't going to worry about the why. The fact that he came to me in search of comfort meant everything. It meant that he still cared about me.

His phone began to ring again as we headed to the kitchen to feed the girls. I prepared mac and cheese and he warmed some wieners for them. He cut the wieners up and put them on a plate and then I added the mac and cheese. We sat the girls at the table in their seats. I placed Nina in Ari's high chair and Dom proceeded to put Ari in her booster chair and strap her in.

As the girls ate, Dom and I sat in silence while we watched them. When they were done, I rustled the girls off to give them a bath while Dom cleaned my kitchen. His phone had been going off so much that he had turned it off while the girls were eating. I smiled as I gave the girls their baths. It made me feel good that he chose me to come to for comfort. He could've gone to any one of his other baby mamas, but he didn't. He came to me and that made me feel special.

After I had given the girls their baths, I got them dressed and then ushered them into Arianna's room. The girls got in bed and I adjusted the protective railing to keep them from falling out of the bed. Dom joined us a short time later and sat down in one of the chairs. I sat in the other chair and grabbed the nursery rhyme book I had purchased to read Ari to sleep. I started reading and 20 minutes later, they were both knocked out. I closed the book and placed it back on the bookshelf. Dom and I walked out of the room, leaving a crack in the door.

We walked back to the living room and sat down on the sofa. It was almost nine o'clock by that time. "Are you alright?" I asked.

"Not really. I mean, how would you feel if your mom was dying?" he asked. I guess the look on his face let him know that he had crossed the line. "I'm sorry. I didn't mean ta say it like dat. This shit was just such a shock, ya know?"

"Yea, I know. It was a shock for me and her too. When she found out, all she did was cry. But, a couple of weeks, she said she made peace with God and was ready to accept her faith," I said.

The look on his face was one of disbelief. "So, you're telling me dat my mom is ready ta die? Is dat what you sayin' ta me?"

"Yea. She went to church and spoke with the pastor and everything. By the time we left, she said she wasn't afraid to die and that if God was ready for her, she was ready to go. She said she was just worried about you taking care of Nina. She was concerned that you wouldn't be able to handle taking care of a child all the time."

"Wait… whatchu mean me taking care of Nina?"

"Well, you are her only sibling. Who else would take care of her once her mom is gone?" I asked.

"Damn. I hadn't even thought about dat shit," he said as he buried his face in his hands.

"It's okay. I'm sure your future wife will be more than happy to help you raise your baby sister," I said with a fake smile.

I knew that April wouldn't want to take care of Dom's little sister. I didn't know how I knew that, but I just had a feeling. Hell, the two of them had been together almost two years and still had no children. I didn't think she was the motherly type.

"It ain't even about dat, Rah. How am I supposed ta tell ma baby sister dat our mom ain't here when she starts cryin' fa her?" he said with tears in his eyes. He began to sob again so I wrapped my arm around his shoulders and pulled him to me. As I held him while he cried, tears began to stream from my own eyes. It was sad to think about Nina growing up without her mom.

I didn't know how my baby would take it if something happened to me, so I understood where Dom was coming from. As the two of us cried while holding each other, I kissed his temple. I didn't know why I did it, probably just to soothe him. But that kiss on the temple led to him kissing me on the lips. At first, I wanted to stop him. I didn't want him to do something he'd regret tomorrow. But his lips felt so good on mine. I still loved Dom and I missed him so much.

As our kiss grew deeper, I could feel my kitty begin to moisten. I pushed him out of my arms slowly. "What's wrong?" he asked.

"I don't want to do something that you'll regret tomorrow or some time down the line. I still love you Dom and I just don't want you to hurt me again." I stood up from the sofa and said, "If you want to stay over, you can sleep on the couch or in the spare bedroom. I'm just gonna turn in. Good night."

With that being said, I walked out of the living room and headed to my room. Once I made it there, I felt the need to take a shower. The bottom half of my body was really heated. I wanted Dom so much, but I didn't want him to look back on what happened as a mistake. I turned the water on and allowed the temperature to warm up. When it was at the desired temp, I undressed and stepped in. As the water rained down on me, I felt my body start to relax.

Imagine my surprise when I felt Dom's hands on me. When he touched me, I jumped because he startled me. I figured he would have stayed on the sofa, but definitely hadn't expected him to follow me in here. He turned me around to face him and I had to bite down on my bottom lip as I took in his physique. Oh my God! He was so fucking sexy.

He placed his hands on both sides of my face and brought his lips down on mine. As our tongues danced in each other's mouths, he pulled me closer to him. I could feel the bulge of his manhood against me and at that point, it didn't matter if he had any regrets tomorrow. We had passed the point of no return and I needed to feel him inside me.

He picked me, pushed my body against the shower wall and thrust his dick inside me. I gasped as his big dick invaded my vaginal sugar walls. I hadn't had sex in almost eight months and oh my God! As he pumped in and out of me, I cried out softly as I hung on to him tightly. He moaned softly as he nibbled on my perky D cup breast. I couldn't believe we were actually having sex in the shower. We hadn't been together in so long, but here we were, engaging in some very sinful activity.

After a couple of more deep thrusts that almost ruptured my G-spot, our bodies shook and trembled as we succumbed to our guilty pleasures. He held me against the wall, kissing me for a few minutes before he removed his pole from my sugar cookie. He placed my feet on the floor and without saying a word, we began to lather ourselves with soap. Several minutes later, we stepped out of the shower and dried ourselves off. We didn't say anything until we were finished.

"I wanna spend the night here," he said as he gazed into my eyes.

"Yea, I told you it was fine."

"In your bed," he said as he took my hand and led me to my room. I gulped at the thought of our long, sleepless night ahead of us. No more words were said as we climbed in my king- sized bed. He immediately went down on me and began to lick my pussy. That was definitely something he had never done to me before. I spread my legs wider as he lapped up my juices like a thirsty dog in his water dish. My legs shook as he rotated his tongue in a circular motion inside me.

"Mmmmmm!" I moaned as he stuffed my vagina with two fingers. As he drove his fingers in and out of me, he continued to lick my clitoris. I slowly began to hump his tongue. After a few minutes, he came up for air as his dick stood at attention. I felt the need to reciprocate the oral pleasure he had given me. As I sat up in the bed, I stroked his hard, stiff meaty pipe.

He moaned as I took it in my mouth and began to suck on it. I gagged a couple of times at first because this wasn't something I was used to. After a few more sucks, my mouth finally adjusted and I stopped gagging. I sucked and sucked until he removed his dick from my mouth. As he pushed me back on the bed, he got between my legs and his dick found its way back inside me. As I wrapped my legs around him, something I couldn't do before, he began to rotate his hips in a circular motion as he worked his dick inside me. I held on to him as our lips connected.

This was a level of intimacy we didn't have before. I didn't understand how we ended up in this situation, but I couldn't have been happier. As his thrusts got harder and more intense, I opened my legs wider to give him what he needed. He pummeled inside me deeply as my toes curled and my body shivered. He kissed me again and asked me to turn over. I gladly got on all fours as he got behind me and inserted his big dick once again.

It felt so good to have Dom inside me again. He was going so deep that my entire insides were quivering. "Oh my God!" I cried out. As my body shook, he smacked my ass, making my orgasm burst out on his dick. "Sssssss!"

He continued to hit it hard from the back as he spread my ass cheeks. I buried my head in the pillow to keep from waking the girls. I hadn't felt this good in a long time. I wasn't sure what was going to happen between Dom and I once this was all over, but if what we were doing was helping him, I didn't mind. I just hoped that he wouldn't toss me to the side like a pair of old socks when this was all over.

After what felt like hours, and after several different positions, he finally released his monstrous orgasm. I was truly exhausted after we were done. I fell onto the plush mattress as he laid beside me. We were breathing heavily as our sweaty bodies slightly touched each other. Not long after that, I heard him softly snoring beside me. I just closed my eyes and went to sleep because he had worn me out.

Chapter twelve

Dominic

After talking to the nurse, I was devastated to hear that my mom was dying. I mean, she was all I had. I didn't know what I was going to do without my mom. When I left my mom's house, I didn't know where to go. I didn't want to go home because I didn't want to hear April talking about the wedding. That was the last thing I wanted to talk about after hearing the bad news about my mom. I ended up at Rasheeda's place because she was the only one who knew what my mom was going through. She would be the only one that would be able to comfort me.

When I arrived, I knocked on the door. When she opened that door, she looked good as fuck. She was wearing some 'come fuck me' shorts, or at least that was what I thought they were saying, and a tank top. As she pulled me into her arms, I inhaled her sweet scent. Once the kids were down, I sort of expected things to get a bit heated between us. Hell, I hadn't fucked in four and a half months. What I didn't expect was for her to push me away because she was worried about me having regrets. I was crushed when she left me sitting there with my dick on hard.

She went into her bedroom and closed her door. I waited to hear the lock click in place, but when it didn't, I made my way there. I turned the knob and found that it wasn't locked, just as I suspected. If she had wanted to keep me out of her room, she would've locked the door. I knew she wanted me there. When I heard the water running in the bathroom, I began to remove my clothes. I turned the bathroom doorknob and it opened. When I saw her silhouette in the shower, I quickly made my way in. When

Rasheeda and I first got together, I never would have tried to pick her big ass up. She was liable to rupture a disc in my back, pull a fucking muscle in my arm or some shit like that.

That was not the case now. She had lost a good 70 pounds or so. She no longer had the shape of that purple blob monster from the McDonald's character. Nah uh. She was built like a glass Coke bottle, but with a little more pow to the rear and cleavage. Rasheeda was fine. I would have been a damn fool if I hadn't picked her up and pinned her against the wall. She felt good in my arms as I held onto her firm ass cheeks. Damn. She must've been doing some squats too. That ass used to jiggle more than a Jell-O mold. Now, it was tight and firm in my hands. I said a prayer before I put my dick inside of her.

"Good Lord, please forgive me because I'm about to act the donkey in this pussy. I know I'm supposed to be getting married and shit, but damn. If you really wanted me to marry April, you woulda neva put me in this situation wit Rasheeda. You knew she was fine. Oh Lawd! I'm bout to beat it up like some egg whites. Lata!"

Several hours later, the two of us crashed on the bed, exhausted from all the sex we had.

*****

I woke up during the night with my dick on hard. I wasn't sure what time it was, but it was still dark outside. I rolled over and grabbed Rasheeda by the waist, kissing the nape of her neck. She moaned softly as I lifted her leg to put my dick inside her soft folds. Her moans became louder as I pounded into her backside. "Oh my God, Dom!" she moaned. "I love you so much."

That shocked me because I didn't think she still had feelings for me. I didn't let that shit stop me from getting that good pussy though. I could tell that she hadn't had sex in a while because her pussy was definitely tight. The grip her pussy had on my dick was so tight it could choke a thoroughbred. That pussy was giving me life right about now. I drove my dick inside until we were both moaning. Her body shook as she came on my dick.

I turned her onto her stomach, straddled her ass, and proceeded to drive my dick inside with such force, she hollered. She quickly bit down on her bottom lip to keep from waking up the girls. I felt her squeezing her vaginal muscles around my dick and I almost lost it. I plowed into her pussy like a well-oiled jack hammer as she struggled to not scream. When I came over to Rasheeda's, I had no intentions on beating up the pussy. I only came by to talk, but I couldn't help myself. I knew she wanted me, especially when I found her in the shower trying to cool off.

As I pulled my dick out of her, I lifted her body off the bed in the doggy style position. I got behind her like a nigga getting ready to propose marriage and proposed to that pussy. I was ready to destroy that pussy. It had been a while since I felt a snug pussy like Rasheeda's wrapped around my dick. As I continued to beat it up from behind, she continued to fight the urge to yell and scream.

By the time we were done, the sun was coming up. I laid next to her, taking deep breaths to steady my breathing. "Oh… my… God!" she said as she lay beside me breathing fast.

"You aight?" I asked.

"I'm just trying to catch my breath. Shit, I don't know if I'll be able to walk straight today," she said.

"You gon' be straight."

"I don't know about that. It's been a long time since I had sex and even longer since I've had great sex."

"Well, I was more than happy to break you off some," I said.

"I'm so exhausted," she said.

"I whooped dat pussy, huh?"

"Boy, shut up!" she said as she laughed.

I laid beside her as I contemplated what I was going to do today. I knew that April was probably wondering where I was, but I wasn't ready to see her yet. As a matter of fact, lying in this bed with Rasheeda let me know that I wasn't ready for marriage either. I just didn't know how I was going to break the news to April.

"Dom?" Rasheeda called.

"Huh?"

"What are you thinking about?"

"Whatchu mean?" I asked.

"I've been trying to get your attention, but you were spaced out. Were you thinking about your mom?" she asked.

"Not really. I mean, knowing what I know got me kinda bummed. But…"

"But what?"

"April is planning a wedding dats supposed to happen in less than two months. I don't know if I can go through wit dat shit, yo."

That was the first time I had said the shit out loud. Of course, I had doubts, but the fact that I loved April was supposed to stand for something, right? I thought I'd be able to go through with it, but now, I didn't know how I could do that. I had been apart from Rasheeda for over a year. I never thought the two of us would be in this situation.

Rasheeda propped herself up on her elbow and looked deep into my eyes. "Why you lookin' at me like dat?" I asked.

"I'm trying to figure out if you're serious."

"C'mon nah, you really think I'd tell you some shit like dat if I wasn't serious?" I asked.

"Wow! You are serious?"

"Hell yea!"

"Well, you better tell her."

"How can I tell her some shit like dat?" I asked.

"How can you not? I mean, what are your choices? You either have to tell her now and give her time to cancel everything, go through with it, or leave her at the altar. I don't think even you're cruel enough to leave her at the altar." When I didn't respond, she looked at me and asked, "Are you?"

"I didn't say all that. I mean, I know I need to tell her. I just don't know how."

How was I supposed to break her heart like that? I chased that girl for six months before she agreed to go on a date with me. She finally agreed and then I proposed. After I proposed, I got extremely nervous, wondering if I could go through with it. I never once wanted to get married. My mom assured me that was the best thing for me. She said that if I loved April, I should go on and marry her. She said that was what all mature men did. Shit, I wasn't mature yet. I was only 24.

"Just tell her the truth, Dom. Trust me, she'd rather hear it from you than hear it from someone else," she said.

I knew that she was right, but I just didn't know how to do that shit. I used to be able to tell women fuck off and just dump them, but I wasn't that nigga anymore. I hadn't even been cheating on April, like talking about it.

"Dom…" Rasheeda said she nudged me.

"Huh?"

"What are you thinking about?"

"I'on know. I'ma get a nap in before the kids wake up," I said as I turned my back. I didn't feel like discussing this shit anymore. I had a lot of thinking to do, about my mom, my little sister, Rasheed and April. Why the hell was my damn life so fucking complicated?

Chapter thirteen

April

Three days later...

Dominic hadn't been home since he left to go see his mom four days ago. I had been calling him, but his phone kept going straight to voicemail. That could only mean that he had turned his phone off. I called his mom, but some lady kept answering her phone. I kept hanging up, but today I was going to ask her about Dom's whereabouts.

"Hello," she answered.

"Ma'am, my name is April, I'm Dominic's fiancée."

"Oh, hello. I'm Jennifer, Ms. Belinda's nurse."

"Her nurse? Is Ms. Belinda okay?" I asked.

"She's really ill."

"What's wrong with her?"

"I'm sorry, but I'm not at liberty to discuss that with anyone but her son or Rasheeda."

What the fuck did she mean, Rasheeda? Rasheeda wasn't marrying Dominic, I was. What the hell did she have to do with his mom or her condition?

"I'm sorry, but I don't understand. What does Rasheeda have to do with this? I mean, her son, I understand, but Rasheeda..."

"She's been helping me take care of Ms. Belinda while her son was away."

"Is he there now?" I asked, hoping and praying that she'd say yes.

"No, he isn't."

"Is she there?"

"No, she isn't."

"Okay, thank you. Can you please tell Ms. Belinda I'll be by to see her soon?" I said.

"I sure will."

We ended the call and I decided to go pay Rasheeda a visit. If she knew what was going on with Dominic's mom, maybe she knew where he was. I had tried calling her multiple times, but she never responded. I mean, she didn't even have the decency to return my call. I mean, what if it was an emergency pertaining to Dominic? He was her baby's daddy, didn't she care? My mind was going crazy with worry about Dom. I just couldn't get over the fact that he hadn't been home in four days. What the hell was he doing? If he wasn't with his mom, where the hell was he?

I knew he wasn't with Tisha because she had a man. I knew he wasn't with his baby mama in Metarie because she lived too far. I knew he wasn't with Ashley because Tory would kick his ass again. And I knew damn well he wasn't with that chick Mariah. He couldn't even stand her. He disliked her so much that the only way he saw his baby girl was if his mom went to pick her up. I had learned from previous discussions that he sometimes dipped back into Trina's, his first baby mama's, kitty. So help me God if I found out that was where he was.

Dom had a notepad with all his baby mama's phone numbers and addresses. That was in case anything happened to him I would be able to get in touch with them to let them know. I made sure to check on them every single weekend just to make sure that they weren't talking to my man while he was gone. I'd be damned if I lose Dom to those hoodrats after everything we have been through. I called Trina, but the phone went to voicemail. I hung up and the phone rang right back.

"Hello," I answered.

"April? What's up?"

"Hey Trina, how are you?"

"I'm good, but I know you ain't call me just ta ask me how I'm doin'. What's up?" she repeated.

"I'm looking for Dominic. Have you seen him?" I asked. To be honest, I was really embarrassed to ask my fiance's baby's mama if she had seen my man.

"I haven't seen Dom in a while. If you happen ta find his ass, tell him his daughter misses him," she said.

"Yea, okay."

We ended the call and I grabbed my keys and headed out the door.

*****

I arrived at Rasheeda's place half an hour later. Dom's truck wasn't in her driveway, but I decided to ask her if she had seen or heard from him anyway.

KNOCK! KNOCK! KNOCK!

I patiently waited for her to answer the door. The door pulled back a couple of minutes later and she stood there with Dom's baby sister on her hip. The grimace on her face told me that she wasn't too happy to see me. I didn't know why she wouldn't be. I thought that the two of us had been getting along great since our first meeting. Maybe I was wrong when I considered us friends.

"Hello," I greeted her.

"Hey, what are you doing here?" she asked.

"Can I come in?"

She moved to the side so I could enter. I walked into her home and followed her into the living room area. She placed Nina down next to Arianna and the two girls played with toys. She and I sat on the sofa and she asked, "Why are you here?"

"I just needed to speak to you and since you weren't answering your phone..."

"You thought you'd just pop up?

"Look, Dominic hasn't been home in a few days and I'm worried about him. When he left the house four days ago, he said he was going to his mother's house because she wasn't feeling well. I've been calling him, but he hasn't answered his calls. I've called his mother's place, but some nurse keeps answering the phone and can't give me any info. The only person she'll give info to are you and Dom. I was just wondering if since she refuses to give me any information, what's going on?" I asked.

"You're Dom's fiancée," she said with a smirk on her face.

"Yes, so?"

"So, if he wants you to know what's going, he'll tell you. I mean, if you really wanted to know what was wrong with his mom, why didn't you just go over to her house?"

"What's with the attitude? I thought that we were cool," I said. I was really shocked by her sudden attitude towards me. I hadn't done anything to her and when Dom was offshore, I always made sure that Arianna had everything she needed. I thought that Rasheeda and I were on great terms.

"I don't have an attitude. I just don't understand what would bring you to my doorstep when you should have gone to Ms. Belinda's house," she said.

"Mommy, I want my dadee!" Arianna whined.

Rasheeda immediately looked uncomfortable, as if she was struggling with what to say next. "Your daddy isn't here Ari," she finally managed to say.

"I want him," Arianna continued to cry.

"Maybe he'll come by later, baby. Just play with Nina," Rasheeda said.

"Has Dom been here since he's been back?" I asked.

"Why would you ask that? I mean, you don't see him, do you?" she asked as she waved her arm around the room.

"I just asked a simple question."

"And I asked you two simple ones."

"Okay," I said as I stood up. "I can see that we're not getting anywhere. I don't know what your issue is with me, but if you happen to see Dom, can you tell him I was here?"

"Yea, sure."

As I made my way to the door, her phone started to ring. She looked at it with this huge smile on her face. Then she looked up at me and asked, "Are you still here?"

"Is that Dominic?" I asked as I crossed my arms over my chest.

"What if it is?"

"What's your problem, Rasheeda?" I really wanted to know what her problem was. I hadn't done anything to this woman. I got along with all Dom's baby mamas' for the past year, including her. Now, all of a sudden, she was giving me nothing but attitude.

"I don't have a problem. I just think you should go look somewhere else to find your man," she said.

I knew she was lying to me. I knew that she was hiding something, but I didn't have time for her bullshit. I didn't know what was going on between her and Dominic, but I sure hoped he wasn't cheating on me. I loved him and I had never once stepped out on him. All I had time to do lately was work and plan this wedding. But, no matter how busy I was, I always made time to check up on his kids for him while he was gone.

That was why I was so confused by Rasheeda's attitude. Before Dom came home, I had called her at least once a week to check up on her and Arianna. I did the same with Tisha, Trina, Rochelle, Mariah, and Ashley. As Dominic's fiancée, I didn't want any beef with his baby mamas. Once he and I got married, we'd all be family anyway. His kids would all be my stepchildren.

I had to pass up our house on the way to his mom's place. When I was passing by our place, I noticed a sheriff's patrol car in the driveway. I pulled alongside him and stepped out of the car. When he saw me, he raised his forefinger for a moment. A couple of minutes later, he stepped out of the patrol car and approached me.

"Hello," he greeted me.

"Hello, can I help you, officer?" I asked confused as to why he was here.

"Is this where Dominic Williams resides?"

"Yes, it is. What is this about?"

"I just have a subpoena for him. Can you make sure that he gets it please?" he asked.

"Subpoena? You mean for court?" I asked.

"Yes ma'am. If you could just sign here please," he said as he gave me a pen. I signed my name on the line and he handed me a yellow envelope with some paperwork. "Have a nice day, ma'am." He turned and got in his car, then backed out of the driveway. More than anything, I wanted to tear open that envelope to see what was inside. But, I knew it was a crime to open someone else's mail and I wasn't trying to go to jail.

I pulled out my phone and dialed his number. I needed to know where he was. As I was ringing his phone, he pulled into the driveway. I pressed 'end' on the phone and waited for him to get out of the truck. He got out and followed me inside the house. The last thing I wanted to do was give our neighbors something to talk about when we were supposed to be happily planning our wedding. I mean, we were getting married in five weeks for crying out loud. What the hell was wrong with him?

After he closed the door, I followed him into the bedroom. I just knew he didn't think that I was going to just let things go after he had been missing for four days.

"Where have you been, Dominic?" I asked.

"Hello to you too, April," he said sarcastically.

"Hello my ass! Where have you been for four damn days?"

"You aren't ma mama. I don't have ta answer ta you," he said as he tried to dismiss me.

"No, I'm not your mama, but I am your fiancée. What's going on with you, Dominic? Is this about the wedding?" I asked. If he didn't want to marry me, he needed to just tell me that. Our wedding was in five damn weeks, so if he didn't want to be my husband, now was the time to say something.

"You still worried about dat damn wedding, huh? It's nice ta know where ya priorities lie," he said.

"What are you talking about? You're my priority!"

"And my mom is mine right now!"

"What's wrong wit your mom?"

"Oh, so now you're concerned about my mom?" he asked.

"Dominic, what's wrong with you? I know that your mom is sick, so please, tell me what's wrong with her. I wanna be here for you, baby," I said as I wrapped my arms around him.

He held me close and started sniffling. Last time I saw him like this; it was because when his friend Slim was killed. I just held him as he sobbed against my shoulder. Then I caught a whiff of perfume on his neck. It was a woman's perfume and it wasn't my scent. I was willing to bet any money that it belonged to Rasheeda. But because he had been MIA for the last four days, I wasn't going to push him.

After a few minutes, he pushed me gently out of his arms. "You wanna talk about it?" I asked.

"My mom has ovarian cancer," he said. That shit blew me away. I didn't even know his mom was that sick.

"Aw, baby. I'm so sorry," I said as I reached for him again. "I didn't know she was that ill. So, are there any treatment options, like chemo or something?"

He shook his head no, and I was wondering if he had even heard me. I knew for a fact that when someone was diagnosed with cancer, there were several treatment plans. "Why are you shaking your head?" I asked.

"There's no treatment. The cancer was caught too late and it spread to some of her major arteries. The doctors are giving her only six months," he said as he broke down again. I had never seen my man that vulnerable before. I bet Rasheeda was enjoying that shit too. She probably couldn't wait to sink her claws into my man.

"I'm so very sorry," I said. "Is there anything I can do?"

He shook his head no again. "Did you hear what I said? My mom's gonna die and there ain't shit nobody can do about it!"

"I didn't know she was that sick," I said.

"Apparently, neither did she."

"I guess that explains why Rasheeda had Nina earlier."

"Yea, she's been taking care of her for my mom the past two or three weeks," he said.

"Wow! How do you know that Nina's been over there for three weeks?" I asked.

"Uh, because she wasn't at my mom's place. DUH!"

"Was that where you were for the past four days… with Rasheeda?"

"Really, April? You gon' really come at me sideways wit dat bullshit after I just told you my mom is dying? You are unbelievable!"

I couldn't believe he was really trying to turn that shit around on me. I had been sitting here for the last four days, worried and concerned about him. Of course, I thought he might have fallen into the clutches of one of his baby mamas. In my heart, I knew he had spent the last few days with Rasheeda and knowing that shit hurt. We were supposed to say, 'I do' in less than two months. I didn't think he was ready at this point. How could he be if he was staying away for days at a time?

"I'm gonna just say this and then I'm done. I'm sorry about your mom, but that doesn't give you an excuse to stay gone for four days without any contact. We're supposed to be married in five weeks, Dominic! FIVE DAMN WEEKS! If you aren't ready and you want things to end, just let me know now! The last thing I want is to be left at the altar by you, so if you don't wanna marry me, tell me now!" I said. I was just tired of this shit. At this point, I didn't even know if I wanted to marry him. I loved him, but I'd be damn if I'd allow him to make a fool out of me the way he did all those other women. "While you marinate on that, here's your mail. The sheriff's office dropped by earlier." I handed him the envelope and walked out of the bedroom and the front door. He had been taken some space for the last few days, now it was my turn.

Chapter fourteen

Tisha

I had heard about Dom's mom being sick and it broke my heart. Over this past year, Ms. Belinda and I had bonded over my kids. Once Dom started acting right, he introduced all of his BM's to her and she was happy to finally spend time with her grandkids. To see that she had a baby as well was a little weird, but my kids and I loved Nina too. I didn't know how Dominic was taking the news, but I imagined that he was devastated. He had expressed to me many times how much he loved his mom. He didn't know his dad and didn't have any brothers or sisters besides Nina, so for him to lose his mom would be extremely hard on him. I could only imagine how he was feeling right about now. And to top it off, he was supposed to be getting married in a few weeks.

My kids were spending the weekend with my mom and Reggie was at work. I decided to give Dom a call and check on him. I hadn't spoken to him since he had been home, and the kids missed him. They hadn't seen him for several months. I hadn't even had the chance to tell him about my engagement to Reggie yet. I dialed his number and waited for him to answer. He finally did on the fourth ring.

"Hello."

"Hey Dom, it's Tisha,"

"Waddup?"

"I heard da news about your mom…"

"News travels fast, huh?" he asked in a sarcastic tone.

"Yea, it does. I was just calling ta check on you. I know dat you weren't expecting ta hear any news like dat," I said.

"I sure wasn't. I'm still trying ta process dat shit."

"I bet. I'm so sorry," I said.

"Thanks. How are da kids? I'm sorry I ain't been around, but wit all dis wedding shit, I been kinda busy, ya know? And now dis shit wit ma mom…" he said.

"Yea, I know you've been busy. The kids are good. They miss you a lot though."

"I miss dem too. I'ma come see dem tomorrow."

"Well, they're spending da weekend at my mom's house. They'll be back Monday though, if you wanna come by then."

"Yea, aight. I'ma do dat," he said.

"Is your mom up for visitors?" I asked.

"Nah, she always tired and shit. I think it's dat medicine they have her on, but I'on know. Maybe, dats cuz of da sickness, ya know?"

"Yea, I know. Just know dat I'll be praying for her."

"Thanks Tisha. I appreciate dat," he said.

"If you need anything, I'm here for you," I said.

"Aight, I'ma holla at you in a couple of days," he said as we ended the call.

I felt a sudden rush of sadness because he sounded so sad. Dom would always be my first love, so I'd always care about him. That didn't mean I was going to fall back into bed with him or anything like that. I loved Reggie and we were happy. There was nothing that Dom could say or do that would make me go back to him. I wasn't the same naïve person I was when I was under Dom's spell. I had grown up and I was a totally different person. I had three beautiful kids, a man who loved me, a job I loved, and I was back in school.

I missed Peaches so much. I often went to visit her mom and Chrissy. Sometimes, I'd pick Chrissy up and we'd all go to the park. Of course, that was when Reggie was off. There was no way I could handle all four kids by myself anymore. They were all big little people with their own little minds. They knew what they wanted and sometimes didn't care whether I liked it or not.

I was lounging on the couch when I got a phone call. I looked at the caller ID and saw that April was calling me. I picked up on the third ring.

"Hey April, what's up?"

"Hey Tisha, how you doing?"

"I'm good, and you?"

"I'm fine. What can I do for you?"

"Just wanted to know if Dominic has been by to see the kids yet?"

"Actually, I just got off the phone with him not too long ago. I was checking on him and Ms. Belinda," I said.

"I know. It's so tragic, huh?"

"Yes, I didn't know she was sick at all. I surely didn't know she had cancer."

"Yea, Dom has been absolutely devastated."

"I'm sure. His mom is all he has besides his kids," I said.

"I know. It's just so sad."

"So, how are the wedding plans going? It won't be long now, huh?" I asked.

"I know, I can hardly believe that in another month, I'll be Mrs. Dominic Williams," she said, but I could tell there was something different in her voice. I mean, she didn't sound as sure about her wedding as she once was.

"You sound really excited. I'm so happy for y'all," I said, and I honestly meant it.

"Thank you so much. Sometimes, I think that Dom has cold feet. I hope that's not the case," she said.

I wouldn't be surprised if he did have cold feet. I mean, Dom was used to being single and spreading that big ol' monster everywhere. No one was more surprised than I was when he said he was marrying April. I mean, he and I had known each other longer and I had three of his kids, but he hadn't asked me to marry him. I just always thought he was rushing things with her, but I'd never tell him that. It wasn't my place.

"I hope not either."

"Well, I was just checking to see how you guys were doing."

I knew she was lying. She was trying to figure out if Dom had been over here. Shit, she didn't have to worry about me and Dom getting it in. I was happily engaged to Reggie. I couldn't wait to marry him.

"We're doing great! As a matter of fact, we're doing better than that because Reg and I are getting married!" I said happily. I mean, if Dominic was having second thoughts about marrying her, I needed her to know that it didn't have shit to do with me.

"What?! You're getting married?!" she practically hollered.

"Yea, Reggie proposed to me a few weeks ago and of course, I said yes."

"Does Dom know?"

I knew that she was worried about Dom and I. I just knew it. Reggie walked in at that moment and I rushed over to give him a kiss. It didn't matter that April was on the phone or not. I needed to greet my man properly.

"Heeellllloooo!" April was calling through the phone line.

"Oh, sorry girl. My man just got back from work. Anyway, in answer to your question, no Dominic doesn't know about our engagement yet because I haven't seen him. However, he did say he would come by to see the kids in a couple of days. When I see him, I'll definitely give him the news," I said.

"Okay, well congratulations! I gotta go," she said.

We ended the call and I went to tend to my man. I hadn't seen him all day and the kids were gone. This was one of those rare times when we were absolutely alone. "Now that I'm done with that, let me greet my man properly," I said as I hugged and kissed my honey bun.

"What was that about?" he asked.

"Nothing that's more important than what we got going on right now," I said as I stuck my tongue in his mouth. He picked me up and I wrapped my legs around his waist as he walked us to the bedroom. I didn't stop kissing him until he put me down. By that time, I could feel his hardened shaft against me.

As he undressed, I did the same. "I want you to sit on my face," he said.

I was more than happy to oblige. My bae had a real good tongue game. It wasn't as fiyah as his dick game though. He laid back on the bed and I straddled his face as I held on to the headboard. As I rode his face, my legs began to quiver. I felt as if my body was in earthquake status. Reggie's tongue was so deep inside me as he circled my wet folds. A short time later, I burst into his mouth, releasing my fluids.

I removed myself from his face and slowly made my way to his erect member. I wasted no time wrapping my lips around it and sucking it. I loved sucking my man's dick and the moans he made let me know that I was doing the damn thang. I continued to slobber on his penis until I couldn't take it anymore. I straddled him and lowered my pussy onto his shaft. It felt so good every time he went inside me. I grinded my pelvis evenly with his thrust and I exploded once again.

"Mmmm!" I moaned as I popped my pussy on his dick.

He gripped my breasts and moaned like a snake as I continued to rotate my hips round and round. Looking at my handsome man as we made love was amazing. I never thought I could love another man like this. The love that I felt for Reggie was different than the love I felt for Dominic. Of course, Dom was my first love and I saw everything through rose colored glasses at that time. Now, that I had my heart broken before, I was a little more guarded with who I gave my love to. But I knew that I had won when I gave it to Reggie. He was the most wonderful man in the world.

He flipped me over and thrust his dick inside me. The two of us were moaning and sweating like a couple of school kids. I couldn't help it though. I was feeling so good, my head was spinning. As he lifted my right leg and placed it on his shoulder, he drove deeper inside me. I was delirious with good feelings as he continued to thrust inside my moistened center. We switched positions so he could take it from the back. That was the one position that really drove me crazy. It was almost as if he had pressed his dick against my G-spot and left it there. The feelings inside me were so intense; I actually opened my mouth and hollered.

The good thing was that no one was here to stop us from getting it in. No kids were in the next room asleep, so I wasn't afraid to wake them. My mom wasn't going to walk in on us or anything like that. It was just me and Reggie, and it showed from the noises we were both making. As he smacked my ass, I continued to throw that ass at him. Finally, after a couple of hours or so, he succumbed to his orgasmic pleasures. He growled like a wolf as he released his fluids inside me. It was at that moment, I collapsed beside him in the bed. I couldn't move even if I wanted to. I was exhausted, to say the least. I was happier than I had ever been in my life.

Chapter fifteen

Tory

Things between Krystal and I had been amazing since we moved in together. The night after Ashley came over and dumped my things at Krystal's I was upset, but happy at the same time. The following day, I went over to Ashley's place to get the rest of my things. I mean, if she had to bring my shit like that, she should've brought all of it. I think she didn't because she wanted me to have a reason to go there the next day. I went at a time I thought she wouldn't be there. I just assumed she was at work. To be honest, I was hoping she wasn't home because I didn't want any kind of arguments.

Three weeks ago…

I arrived at the house and saw her car in the driveway. I rolled my eyes and let out an exasperated breath because I knew shit was about to go left. I walked in, using my key, and she was standing right by the door. "What are you doing here, Tory?" she asked with her hand on her hip.

"I didn't come ta fight or argue witchu. All I came here for was ta get the rest of ma shit."

"So, you really leaving me, huh?"

"Leaving you? Nah, you put me out, remember?" I asked.

"I brought yo shit over there to get yo attention!"

"Well, you got it!"

So, now she had tears in her eyes, but I wasn't going to let that phase me. Her tears were her own. I mean, when she threw me out, that was an escape for me. I needed her to do that because I was struggling to do it myself. I made my way to our bedroom and grabbed my duffle bag set. "You're really doing this?" she asked.

"You put me out! Did you really think dat I was just gonna come back and act like nothing happened?" I asked.

"I didn't think you would just leave me."

"Look, I don't wanna get into an argument while da kids are sleeping..."

"They're with my mom, so you ain't gotta worry about dat," she retorted.

"I'm just tryna get ma shit and be out, ya heard me?"

"I hear you, but don't you even wanna talk about it?" she asked.

"Talk about what? This relationship was doomed as soon as you slept wit ma boy! I tried ma best ta make it work because I wanted ta be around ma son. But I can't keep fighting witchu like dat," I said.

"I don't wanna fight witchu! I love you! How many times do you want me ta say I'm sorry?"

"You can say it until da cows come home. Dat ain't gon' change da fact dat you slept wit ma best friend. Not only did you sleep wit him, but you planned da whole gotdamn seduction. Tell me somethin', Ashley, did you even think about me when you did dat shit? I mean, things

between us were good, right? So, why? You never once answered dat question."

"Dats because I don't know why I did it. I wish I could tell you, but I don't know!"

"And dat right there is why we can't be together. In yo heart, you felt like we couldn't or shouldn't be together..."

"I neva thought we shouldn't be together!" she cried.

"Yea, you did. Otherwise, you would never have taken yo clothes off ta fuck ma best friend!" I said.

"I'm sorry... I'm sorry! How many more times..."

"You ain't gotta say it no mo'! It don't even matter. It ain't gon' change nothin'. You still fucked him and you still had a baby wit him!" I said. I watched as she continued to cry and sob, but there wasn't shit I could do. I wasn't here to comfort her or make her feel better. I only came to get my shit and be out. I was hoping my son was here so I could see him before I left, but I'd just have to see him another time.

"What about our boys?" she asked.

"I love Kyon, but he ain't ma son. I've managed ta bond wit him because of how much time Dom spent offshore, but he ain't mine. No matter how much I wish he was, he ain't. I hope I won't have ta go through the courts ta see Keenan," I said.

"I'd never keep you from your son, but I don't want him around dat bitch!"

"She's not a bitch! She's the mother of my child, and you will respect her!"

"Respect the bitch who took my man from me? Hell no!" she said.

"You will respect her because she is gonna respect you!"

"I still don't want ma son..."

"OUR SON! And as long as I ain't puttin' him in no danger, you have nothin' ta worry about," I said.

I began throwing my things in my bags. I watched as she cried bloody murder, but that wasn't my problem. I would always care about Ashley, but we'd never be together again. When I had packed up all my stuff, I told her, "You can keep da furniture. Because I'm on da lease, I'ma continue ta pay ma half until da year is up. When da lease runs out, I'ma start payin' you fa child support. Then you gon' have ta find somethin' you can afford."

"I love you, Tory. I'll always love you," she said.

"I'll always love you too, but as the mother of my son, nothin' more, nothin' less."

I grabbed my stuff and took it out to the car. She followed me outside and I wondered what she did that for. I mean, why did she need to follow me out here. "Please don't leave me, Tory! I'll do anything!"

"Stop making a fool of yourself out here in front of these damn nosy ass neighbors! I'm gon' co-parent witchu, but we are done! Please don't make this shit harder than it need ta be," I said.

She wrapped her arms around me and continued to sob on my shoulder. "C'mon, man. I ain't tryna do this shit in front all these people," I said as I tried to push her off of me.

"I love you, Tory. Don't leave me! PLEASE!" she cried.

"Dammit, Ashley! Stop doing this shit!" I finally managed to get her off of me. I got in my car and drove off. I felt bad about hurting her feelings. I mean, I probably felt worse than she did when she fucked Dom. But, I wasn't basing my happiness on how happy she was anymore. It was time for me to live for Tory.

Present day...

I had plans to go pick my son up today. I was actually picking both of the boys up and we were going to go chill with Dom in the park. I hadn't spent much time with him since he had been back, but I knew he was going through a lot. I didn't know what I'd do if my mom was dying. I knew he was taking it hard because his mom was the only one that raised him. He also seemed stressed about his upcoming wedding. I personally didn't think that he was ready to get married, but he still hadn't called off the wedding. I had nothing against April, but I just didn't think that Dom was the marrying type. I figured he might be going through with it because Slim and Peaches were planning to get married when they were killed.

Slim's death really hit Dom hard. It seemed that since Slim died, he had turned over a new leaf. He was doing everything according to how he thought Slim would do it. I was going to talk to him and tell him that it was okay to be himself. He had to do what was right for him and no one else.

As I was getting dressed to go pick up the boys, Krystal was getting dressed for work. She worked at AT&T, so she couldn't be late. "Babe, is Keenan spending the night?" she asked.

"I hadn't thought about it. Why?"

"I thought it would be nice if he and I spent some time together. I mean, I am with his daddy and we are having a baby," she said.

"Well, by da time you get off, he'll be asleep. I'll get him da next time we're both off and we can take him to Chuck E. Cheese's or somethin'."

"Okay, I love you," she said.

"I love you too, babe. Be careful," I said as we kissed.

"I am so lucky to have you. Do you know I wake up every morning thanking God for bringing you into my life?"

"No, I didn't know dat."

"It's true though. I never thought dat I could be this happy," she said.

I wrapped my arms around her and held her close as I stroked her hair. "I'm blessed to have you too, babe. Now, you better getcho fine ass outta here. You know AT&T don't play dat shit!"

We kissed again and she left. I grabbed my keys and left right behind her. It didn't take me long to get to Ashley's place. Thankfully, she had the boys all ready when I got there. I was glad because I didn't want to have to wait while she got them ready. She helped me strap the boys in and asked me not to be too late getting them back. After they waved by to her, I backed out the driveway.

I hit up Dom to make sure he was on his way. Imagine my surprise when he said he was bringing Rasheeda, Arianne, and Nina with him. I didn't know what the hell he was doing, but I wasn't going to say anything about it.

I arrived at Chuck E. Cheese's first and got the boys out. Once we were inside, I ordered the pizza and got the tokens. While we waited for the pizza, I took the boys to the play area. While I watched them play, Dom and Rasheeda walked over with the girls. The girls immediately jumped in the ball pit with the boys.

"S'up Rasheeda?" I greeted.

"Nothing much, Tory. How've you been?" she asked me.

"I've been aight. You?"

"Better than alright," she smiled as she shoulder bumped Dominic. "I'm gonna go play wit the kids so you guys can talk about me."

She walked away and I watched as Dom's gaze followed her ass. When she was out of earshot, I asked, "Wassup, bro? How's your mom?"

"She's hanging in there. Man, I neva thought I'd see ma mom so weak and shit. You know, as a kid we think our parents are invincible and shit. When we get older, we still think of them as some kind of super hero. But da truth is, they just regular folks. I hate seeing her like dat and they ain't got shit I can do about it," he said as his eyes teared up. I couldn't imagine how he was feeling right now.

"I'm sorry ta hear dat, bro. I've been keepin' her in ma prayers," I said.

"Thanks."

"On another note, whatchu you doin' here with Rasheeda? Don't tell me… you called off the wedding and the two of y'all are back together."

"Nah, the wedding still on," he said as he rubbed his chin.

"Say what? You still gettin' married ta April, even though you here with Rasheeda?"

"Me and Rah have a child together."

"So, y'all ain't sleeping together?" I asked.

"Well…"

"I knew it! Does April know?"

"Hell no! She don't know shit! Look man, da truth is dat Rah been here fa me. She was there fa ma mom, and she's been lookin' after Nina. Dats some shit dat April shoulda been doin', but she wasn't."

"So, why you still planning on marrying her?" I asked.

"Man, we spent a lotta money on dat damn wedding! If I don't marry her, we gon' lose all dat money!"

"So, you marrying her so you don't lose yo money?"

I was surprised that he would be still be planning to marry April just so he didn't lose the deposits and shit. Damn. That was some bullshit!

"Hell yea! I coulda spent dat money on ma child support! You remember dat chick we saw on Bourbon dat night?"

"Who? Da one who said she had a kid by you?"

"Yea, her."

"What about her?" I asked.

"I got a subpoena for child support."

"What?! Another subpoena?"

"Yep. Got to court and I asked the judge for a paternity test," he said.

"Right! I remember you said he belonged to the milk man," I said.

"Yea, I got whole and low fat... which one you want?" he asked.

"Da fuck? The kid is yours?"

"Yea!"

I almost fell out my seat laughing so hard at Dom's ass. I had a feeling that was his kid, but he had to find out for himself. Damn. That nigga had nine kids now...

Chapter sixteen

Rasheeda

When Dom left that day to go home and tend to his business, I knew I hadn't seen the last of him. When he showed up on my doorstep that night, I was happy as fuck. Not only did he choose me to share his problems with, but he also chose me to make love too. From the fast nut he busted the first time, I could tell that I was the first to get it since he had come back home. That meant everything to me. I loved Dominic before that lil white bitch even came on the scene. It didn't matter to me one bit that she was planning a wedding with him. I didn't think he'd ever go through with it.

When she showed up at my house at the end of the week, Dom had just left to go visit with his mom. How did she even figure it was okay to just show up at my house? I had never just dropped by her place. As a matter of fact, I had never even been there before. She had a lot of nerve coming to me looking for Dominic. But shit, had she come about 20 minutes before, she would have found him right between my fucking legs where he belonged.

Over the course of the past three and a half days, Dominic and I had engaged in so much sex, it should have been a crime. I hadn't had sex in eight months, so when he first entered inside me, I couldn't breathe for a couple of minutes. But it didn't take me long to get with it though. He even let me ride that big thang cowgirl style and boy did I ride. I rode that sucka like those cowboys on that old *Bonanza* western. When he said he was going to check on his mom, I was a little relieved because that gave me the opportunity to soak my kitty in the tub. She really needed to relax her muscles for a bit. But April had shown up before I had the chance to soak.

Shit, I was surprised she didn't smell the sex on me since I had just finished riding "her man." That shit was just too funny. She really thought Dominic was her man. I wanted so badly to burst her little bubble, but I was going to let Dom do that shit.

After I finally got rid of her ass, my mom came by to get the girls to take them to the park. That was when I decided to sit in the tub. I had some quality time to think to myself and I wondered where this thing between Dom and I was headed. I still loved him and wondered if he loved me too. I didn't want to push for too much too soon though, especially since he had unfinished business with April's ass. What did he see in her anyway?

As I stood in the mirror and gazed at my nude reflection, I smiled at the image I saw. I was finer than April. My titties were bigger than hers. My ass had shaped nicely with the squats that I had been doing. She had a small booty compared to mine, and I knew for a fact that Dom loved my ass. He always made sure to grab both handfuls of it every chance he got. I hadn't seen him since that afternoon he left to go see his mom. That was about three weeks ago.

He and I had been talking on the phone though and I was still visiting his mama. Ms. Belinda and I had bonded over the past six months and I felt as if I was losing my stepmom or something. The cancer had taken its toll over her the past couple of weeks. Her body was brittle and now she had a catheter bag because she was too week to get out of bed. She often ate soup and broth because she was just so weak. I knew she wasn't going to last much longer and I hated that. I hated that this sickness had claimed her that way. I loved Ms. Belinda. She was a very special woman to me and it saddened me to see her like that.

When Dominic called to see if I wanted to come with him and take the girls to Chuck E. Cheese's, I wanted to decline. However, I thought it would be a good outing for the girls, so I agreed. He came by to pick us up and we got the girls in their car seats and climbed in the front seats. I didn't know whether to hug or kiss him since it had been three weeks since we last seen each other.

"How you been?" I asked.

"Aight, I guess. What about you?" he asked.

"Okay, but I missed you."

He looked over at me and smiled. "Yea?"

"Yea." I smiled back at him.

"I missed you too," he finally admitted.

"Fa real?" I asked.

"Real talk."

"So, why haven't you come by the last three weeks?"

"Man, so much shit been going on. April still planning da wedding…"

"You're not still going through with it, are you?" I asked. My heart was beating a mile a minute as I waited for him to respond. I would've thought with everything that had happened between him and I, he would've canceled that farce of a wedding.

"I know you don't wanna hear this shit, but I got ta go through wit it," he said.

"What? After everything that happened between us?"

"I gotta do it, ma. I mean, dat fuckin' wedding cost ma ass an arm and both ma damn legs. If I don't go through wit it, all ma money gon' be lost and I ain't finna give these white people all ma fuckin' bread fa nothin', yo."

I'd be lying if I said that wasn't breaking my heart. I thought that he would've broken off the engagement with April and come back to me. I guess that was stupid on my part. I didn't even realize that I had a tear that had slipped away until he brushed it away.

"Don't cry, Rah. I swear, I don't wanna hurt you."

I looked up into his eyes and saw sincerity in them. He had never looked at me the way that he was looking at me right now. I took his hand from my face and kissed it. "I don't want you to marry her," I said softly.

"I know you don't. Like I said, we spent a helluva lotta money puttin' dat shit together, so I gotta do it."

"That's not a reason to get married, Dom."

"It's ma reason," he said.

"What about us?" I asked.

"Rah, you've been there for me in ways I can't even begin to explain. I care about you so much. This shit with April don't have shit ta do wit me and you," he said.

"How can you say that, Dom? Once you married her, you'll be her husband. Then what?"

"Then I don't know. I haven't figured all dat shit out yet. I also just found out I got another kid, so my mind…"

What the fuck did he just say? He found out he got another kid? What other kid?

"Wait a minute. Pump your brakes. What are you talking about, Dominic? What other kid?" I asked.

"This chick I used ta fuck wit back in da day had a kid, my kid, and I just found out about it," he admitted.

"Oh my God! How did you find out?"

"She told me, then she tried to put me on child support, so I asked for a DNA test. Da shit came back positive, so I have another son."

"Wow! Have you seen him yet?"

"Yea, a couple of times. He's a cool lil kid. His name is Cameron, he's four years old and a lighter version of myself, which is why I didn't think he was mine," he said.

"Wooooow! You told April yet?" I asked.

"Nope. You're the first person I told."

There he went making my heart all mushy again. For him to share something so personal with me before his "fiancée" meant that he cared more about me, right? Well, that was how I was going to look at it. I leaned over and planted a kiss on his lips.

"What was dat for?" he asked as he smiled.

"For sharing that information with me first. You made me feel special," I said.

"You are special ta me, Rasheeda. I wished I hadn't treated you da way dat I did back then. We'd probably still be together," he said, which made my heart swell even more.

"You know I still love you, right?" I asked.

He pulled into the parking lot, found a spot, and turned off the truck. He looked over at me and said, "Yea, I know. I wish I could tell you that back, but in the situation I'm in right now, I don't want to fuck with anybody's emotions. Ya feel me?"

I did understand what he was saying, but I wished he would tell me that he loved me. I also knew that if he said those three words, I'd never let him go through with that damn wedding, no matter how much he spent.

"I feel you. I'm glad we had this talk. I still don't think you should marry that woman just because of money issues. You should marry someone because you love them. I don't think you love her. I think you fell for her because she wasn't putting out so easily. That is what attracted you to her. Don't make that mistake and marry that girl," I pleaded.

"Mommeeeee! I wanna play!" Arianna whined from the back seat.

I leaned in and gave her daddy a kiss on the lips. "I love you." Then I hopped out the truck and got Arianna out while he got Nina. The four of us headed inside and I almost dropped my baby when I saw Tory.

"I didn't know Tory was gonna be here," I said.

"Yea, he invited me because he was bringing the boys. But guess what?"

"What?"

"He didn't know you was comin' either," he said as he cracked up.

Well, if he invited me after Tory invited him, maybe he had told Tory about us. Shit, I felt like Wonder Woman now. I knew if Tory knew, he'd be able to talk Dom out of marrying April's ass. I excused myself just so they could talk about me and Dom. I was confident by the time we left here this evening; Dom was coming home with me for good.

Chapter seventeen

Dominic

Two days before the wedding...

I couldn't believe that in two days, I'd be a married man. I knew that I was getting married for the wrong reasons, but I'd figure that shit out later. Right now, April had spent well over $20,000 for this wedding and because the deposits and shit were non-refundable, I had no choice but to go through with it. I stood in the tuxedo shop trying on the tux. That shit fit me good as fuck. I felt like the dude Quincy on *The Best Man* and I was gonna do just what he said, "pimp that bitch." I looked so good in this muthafuckin' tux.

Tory, Shane and three other friends of mine were also getting fitted for their tuxedos.

"You look very hot in that tux, Mr. Williams," the sales chick complimented.

"Thank you," I said.

"Dom, I still can't believe you bout ta marry dat girl. You shoulda just called off da wedding," Tory said.

"Call off da wedding?!" Shane asked excitedly. "What da fuck did I miss?"

"Nothin'. Just Dom being Dom. Da nigga don't wanna get married, but he gon' go through wit it because he don't wanna lose out on dat money he spent," Tory explained.

"Da hell?! You finna marry dat girl because of all da money you spent?" Shane asked.

"We spent a lotta fuckin' money, most of it was mine!"

"Dats da wrong reason ta get married, man," Shane said.

"Dats what I said," Tory co-signed.

"Look, I know dat ain't da right reason ta say I do, but there's 20,000 reasons why I need ta say it," I said.

"So whatchu gon' do after y'all get married? You don't really wanna go through wit it, so how you think dats gon' work out?" Tory asked.

"I'on know, man. I'ma figure dat shit out when we get back from da honeymoon," I said.

"Y'all going on a honeymoon too?" Shane asked.

"Yea, them ppl at da bar she work at, and some of the customers, all pitched in and got us five days in da Virgin Islands. I had ta get a passport and everything," I said. I had never been out of the country before, but I was looking forward to going to the Virgin Islands. The brochures that we were given when we went to the travel agency were beautiful. I had never seen bluish green water or white sand beaches before, so that was something I was looking forward to.

"Wow! Dats nice. I still don't think y'all should get married though," Tory said.

"Yea, me either. People should get married because they love each other," Shane said.

"Damn, we look good as fuck in these tuxedos!" I said. The six of us stood in the mirror admiring our reflections. We looked good. Shit, if I had known I had looked this good in a tux, I would have gotten one a long time ago.

"Hell yea, we look good!" Brian said.

"Let's get outta here. I got a couple of more errands to run," I said.

We all headed to the dressing rooms and got changed, paid for the tuxedos and were out the door. As I was getting in my truck, my phone started ringing. "Alright fellas! I'ma holla at y'all lata!"

My bachelor party was tomorrow night and I couldn't wait. April was calling me though, so I picked up. "Whaddup?"

"What are you doing?"

"I was getting my tux wit da fellas. Why?"

"Are you coming home now?" she asked.

"Well duh! I gotta come drop off ma tux. Why you askin' all dem questions?"

"I was just trying to see you before I left to go to Renee's house. You know I'll be there until our wedding day," she said.

How could I forget that shit? I was waiting on her ass to leave, so I could be out too.

"Did Trina pick up Bre's dress?" I asked. Bre was going to be the flower girl for the wedding. I had paid for her flower girl dress, but Trina had to go pick it up from the dress shop.

"Yea, she came to pick it up while we were there, so I could see how it fit her. She's going to be such a beautiful little flower girl," April gushed.

"Yea, I know. Well, look, I'm on ma way home, so I'ma see you when I get there."

"Okay, be careful."

"Always."

I hit the 'end' button on the steering wheel and continued to drive towards our house. I arrived about a half hour later, parked my truck, and grabbed my tuxedo. I walked in the house to find April waiting for me. "Hey," I greeted her and kept walking.

She followed me into the bedroom. "Babe, please tell me you're only acting this way because you're nervous about the wedding," she said.

"I ain't nervous about da wedding. I can't wait ta get dat shit ova wit. I'm worried about ma mom and how I'm bout ta lose her. I woulda been happy just going ta da justice of da peace. This shit right here, this big ass show, ain't fa nobody but you," I said.

"Are you upset with me about something?"

"Nah, I'm cool."

She walked over to me and said, "Babe, I know you're worried about your mom. I'm worried about her too."

Now, I knew that shit was a lie. All she had been worried about lately was this damn wedding. She was having her bachelorette party tomorrow night too. She wanted us to have our parties together, but I wasn't having that shit. I wanted a bachelor party with strippers and shit. I didn't want to share my party with April at all.

"Just know that I'm here for you and I love you," she said as she wrapped her arms around my waist. I gave her a hug since that seemed to be the quickest way to get her out of here. She moved out of my arms and gave me a kiss. "If you want me to stay with you, I will."

"Hell naw! Go head on and do yo thang, girl!" I said, anxious to get her out of here.

"Okay, just hit me up if you need me. Otherwise, I'll see you at the altar day after tomorrow."

She finally left and I jumped in the shower. By the time I got out, my phone was ringing. I rushed to see who was calling and picked up. "Hey," I answered.

"Hey babe, what are you doing?" Rasheeda asked.

"I just got out of da shower. What you up to?"

"I was hoping to see you later," she said.

"Where da girls at?"

"They're sitting right here playing."

"Oh, I thought yo mom had them. You know how loud yo ass be gettin' when I'm deep in dem guts," I said.

"No, they're here."

"Aight. I'm finna hit da bar with the fellas, but I can come by later. It might be late though," I informed her.

"Okay, do you have your key?" she asked.

"Of course, I have ma key. I'ma use it too."

"Don't lie."

"I ain't lyin' guh! I'm comin' get some of dat good pooh-na-naaayyy!" I said as we cracked up laughing.

"You so crazy," she said and I could tell she was blushing.

"I'ma see you lata."

"Okay, have fun."

"Sshhiidd! I plan ta do just dat," I said.

"Don't fuck no bitches!" she warned.

"I ain't."

"Love you," she purred.

"Bye bae."

I ended the call and smothered my body with lotion before splashing some cologne on. Then I got dressed and headed out the door. My phone started ringing when I got in the truck and the display on the console said it was Tisha. I hadn't spoken to her in a few days. I went by there to visit my kids last week and she told me that she and Reggie were engaged. I was really happy for her. She seemed very happy and more importantly, my kids were happy. They really loved Reggie and as far as I could tell, he was a great second daddy to them.

"Hey, waddup, Tee Tee?"

"Hey Dom, I know you're probably busy, but I wanted ta call you before things got too hectic," she said.

"Shit, things been hectic!"

"I imagine. I just wanted ta congratulate you and April…"

"I thought y'all was coming ta da wedding," I said.

"We were gonna come, but da twins aren't feeling too good, so we're going ta keep them home. I'm so sorry, but I know it's gonna be beautiful."

"Ssshhhiiddd! It better be a celebrity wedding wit all da money I spent," I said.

"Well, take a lot of pictures."

"How da hell I'm supposed ta do dat?"

"Not you personally, silly!"

"Oh, aight. Thanks fa calling. Tell ma babies I'ma come by and visit when I get back from ma honeymoon," I said.

"Okay. Talk ta you soon," she said as we ended the call.

I arrived at the bar, where me and my friends prepared to enjoy the night.

*****

We finally left the bar around 1:30 the next morning. When a nigga said he enjoyed himself, that was exactly what I did. I didn't fuck nobody at the bar, but I was about to though. I couldn't wait to get all up in between Rasheeda's thighs. I was a little tipsy, but it was okay. I knew how to drive without getting in no damn accident. I put all my windows down on my truck and blasted my damn music to keep my ass awake. I made it to Rasheeda's house a little after two, and thank God, I made it there safely. I parked my truck, chirped the alarm, and used my key to get inside.

I locked the door and took my shoes off before making my way to her bedroom. I stumbled a couple of times on the way, but thankfully, I didn't wake the girls. I crept into Rasheeda's bedroom and took off every piece of clothes I had on. I struggled to get the rope chain off, but eventually, I laid it on the nightstand next to my phone. I climbed in bed and began to kiss on Rasheeda's lips. It didn't take long for her mouth to open to receive my tongue. She surprised me by being butt ass naked. She used to be too shy to sleep without any clothes on, but I was glad she wasn't shy anymore.

I quickly mounted her and stuck my hard dick inside her. Her legs widened as she moaned and I went to work. I was sucking on her titties and penetrating that pussy like a pro. I got on my knees and placed both of her legs on my shoulders as I drove my dick into her wet kitty, deep and hard. "Oh my God!" she cried out. "Sssssshhiiit!"

I continued to slaughter that pussy until I needed to hit it from the back. She turned over and I quickly slid my dick back inside her wet folds. I gripped her hips and pounded inside her, our sweaty flesh sounding like slabs of beef being thrown together in a meat market. She buried her face in the pillow while I went to work on digging inside those guts like I promised. I grabbed her hair and pulled her face out the pillow. She started moaning loud as hell, but I wanted to hear that shit. I wanted to know that she was enjoying this dick down that I was putting on her.

"You love this dick, baby?" I asked.

"Y-y-y-y-y-yaaazzzz!" she stuttered.

"You love da way I fuck you?"

"Oh God, yes!"

I released her hair because I was close to busting a nut. I was really about to put in some work now. I took my dick out of her and got on the floor, pulling her toward me in the doggy style position. When she was to the end of the bed, I got back between her legs and thrust my dick inside her again. Being that my feet were firmly planted on the floor, I was able to hit that pussy harder than before. Now, she was screaming into the pillow, but I couldn't stop. I pummeled that pussy as hard as I could until I finally released. Her body trembled as she released as well. She slowly moved to her spot in the bed and I climbed in next to her.

She laid her head on my arms while our breathing slowly came back to normal. Before I closed my eyes to fall asleep, I heard her whisper how much she loved me.

My wedding day...

The bachelor party last night was off the hook. It was a good thing that my wedding wasn't until two o'clock in the afternoon; otherwise, April would've stayed at that altar waiting on me. I opened my eyes and grabbed my phone on the nightstand to check the time. It read 11:15 AM. I snuggled closer to Rasheeda, since the girls stayed at her mom's last night, and plunged my dick inside her from behind. She whimpered and picked up her leg. I held her leg up as I punished her pussy while we laid on our sides. She moaned louder as I plunged deeper. Her pussy started to make sloshy sounds as I continued to go in and out.

I rolled on my back and pulled her with me. She was now in the reverse cowgirl position and I watched my dick slide in and out of her as she rode slowly. She grinded into my pelvis, tightening her vaginal muscles, which always made my toes curl. That shit felt amazing.

Finally, after several different positions and her busting several orgasms, I succumbed to the pressures of my dick. I busted open like an over exhausted hot water heater. I removed my dick from inside her and quickly went to the bathroom. After taking a piss, I turned on the water and hopped inside. Rasheeda joined me a minute later and the two of us kissed passionately. That was probably the most passionate kiss I had ever shared with a woman. My dick was starting to stand up again, but I knew I was pressed for time.

As she and I continued to kiss, I thought, what the hell! I pressed her back against the shower wall, lifted her up, and wrapped her legs around my waist. I reinserted my meaty pipe inside her as she wrapped her arms around my neck. "I love you, Dominic," she murmured in my ear.

Damn. I knew she was tired of telling me she loved me and not hearing it back. I just didn't want to tell her that shit just yet, especially when I was about to marry April in a couple of hours. "I love you so much," she said as she sniffled.

Aw shit! I didn't mean to make her cry. I pressed my lips against hers as we kissed. I continued to penetrate her until our orgasms melded into one. I slowly removed my dick as we stared into each other's eyes while the water rained down on us. "I love you," I said.

I swear, I meant that shit. She smiled and said, "Please don't marry April today."

I placed her feet on the floor and asked, "What you want me to do? Just lose out on all da money I spent?"

"Yes, take the lost and be happy you found true and real love with me, Dom. I love you so much and now that I know you love me, how can I possibly stand by and watch you marry her?" she asked. I could see the pain in her eyes and I wanted to stay with her, but I couldn't. I didn't care if April and I had to get our marriage annulled after today, I had to go through with this wedding.

I invested too much fucking money in it to just walk away. I lost enough money every month paying child support, not that I was complaining. I understood that it was my responsibility to take care of my kids. But I couldn't afford to lose that money.

"You don't have to watch me, Rah. You can go to your mom's place and spend the day with her and the girls. Don't come to the wedding," I said. I turned around and lathered myself up, then rinsed it off. I had to go by my place to get dressed. Rasheeda was still in the shower crying and that shit hurt me, but I had to do what I had to do.

I threw my clothes on and rushed out of her house. I hopped in my truck and made my way to my place. It was already 12:45. I was supposed to meet the guys at the hotel at one o'clock. I wasn't going to be on time. The plan was for all of us to meet at the hotel, where the wedding was taking place, and we'd get dressed there. I just didn't have time. Rasheeda lived 45 minutes from my place and the hotel was 45 minutes from my place. Damn.

I pulled into the driveway 30 minutes later. I rushed inside and took care of my hygiene. I brushed my teeth, applied lotion, sprayed cologne, and cleaned my ears before I put the tuxedo on. My phone was blowing up, but I didn't have time to answer it. I hoped Rasheeda would take my advice and not come to the wedding. I didn't know if I'd be able to go through with it if she showed up in tears. I didn't know when I fell in love with Rasheeda, but I did. I couldn't blame myself either because she was always looking out for my mom, even while I was home.

She had to put the girls in daycare, so she could go to work. But every day, after she got off work, she always stopped by to check on my mom before picking up the girls. My mom didn't want Nina seeing her that way, so we stopped bringing her over. But Rasheeda and I always made it there at the same time every day to spend time with my mom. I hadn't seen her today or yesterday because of all the shit I had going on, but I'd make sure to see her tomorrow. We weren't scheduled to leave for the honeymoon until the day after tomorrow. I'd make sure my mom was okay before we left.

I finally got dressed and pulled into the hotel parking lot at 1:52 that afternoon. As I headed to the elevator, I got stopped by Tory before I could get on. He and the other groomsmen came rushing up to me.

"Where da hell you been, man? We've been calling you all morning!" Tory said.

"Yea, well, I'm here now. Let's get this show on da road," I said as we headed to the area we were supposed to wait in to start walking down the aisle. I had to walk ahead of them to take my place at the altar. As I starred at all of the women's expression on their faces they could take it all in because I knew I looked good. When I got to the altar, I smiled with the pastor who was officiating the wedding. "Aye, Pastor John, I need you ta do me a favor."

"What can I do for you, Dominic?" he asked in a voice barely above a whisper. The ceremony had started and the groomsmen and bridesmaids began their walk to the altar.

"Look, I'ma need fa you ta eliminate that part where you ask if anybody objects," I said with a smile.

"Excuse me?" he asked with a confused look on his face.

"I don't want you asking if anybody objects. Just get straight ta da 'I do' so we can be out, ya feel me?" I asked.

The last thing I needed was for Rasheeda to stand up and start talking shit at the wedding. If she would do that, it would piss me off because I needed to get my money's worth. I smiled when I saw my baby girl walking with her little flower basket. She sat next to her mommy once she made it up the aisle. Cameron was also in the wedding as my ring bearer. I was glad when Shawna said he could be in the wedding. I still hadn't told April that Cameron was my son, but I just never had the time. Everyone stood as April prepared to walk down the aisle.

Our wedding was being held in the courtyard of the hotel. The gazebo was decorated nicely with flowers to match the bouquets. I would be lying through my teeth if I said April wasn't a beautiful bride. She was very pretty in her form fitted mermaid dress. She didn't have anyone to walk her down the aisle, so she walked by herself. She had tears in her eyes as she made her way to me.

When she got to the altar, she smiled at me. I wanted to ask her why the heck she was crying. This was supposed to be a happy occasion, so what the hell was she crying for. Pastor John started the ceremony, but before he got to the vows, Rasheeda came running through the courtyard. I shook my head because I just knew she was about to start some shit. April looked at me, her eyes full of questions.

"DOM!" Rasheeda cried.

"What the heck are you doing, Rasheeda?" April asked.

My words were stuck in my throat and I couldn't get them out. "Shut up, April! I ain't here for you!"

"Are you really so desperate to keep Dominic that you'd walk up in here to ruin my wedding?" April asked. "You're pathetic!"

"Dom, I've been calling you!" she said.

"Uh, I'm kinda in da middle of somethin'," I responded.

"It's your mom!" Rasheeda said.

The look on her face let me know that it was serious.

Chapter eighteen

Rasheeda

I was beside myself with the thought of Dom marrying that bitch, April. He didn't even love her anymore. He had finally admitted to me that he loved me, but he was still going to go through with the wedding. I had planned on going, but after he told me that he loved me, I couldn't do it. I knew that when the pastor would have asked if anyone objected, I would've jumped up and said I did. I was on my way to my mom's house when I got a phone call from Jennifer, Ms. Belinda's nurse. She said that she had been trying to reach Dom, but he wasn't picking up.

"He's getting married today, Jennifer. Is there anything you need?" I asked.

"Oh my God! I didn't want to tell you this over the phone..."

"Tell me what? Is Ms. Belinda okay?" I asked. My heart began to beat furiously because I was so nervous about what she was going to say.

"She passed away," she said and I could hear in her voice that she was crying.

"WHAT?!" I cried as I pulled my car over.

"She passed away."

"WHEN?!"

"About an hour ago, I went to give her some medication. I thought she was sleeping until I got closer to her. She wasn't breathing, so I immediately dialed 9-1-1.

They were trying to talk me through CPR and I tried, I swear I did. I just couldn't get her to breathe. When the paramedics finally got here, they said there was nothing they could do."

"Oh my God!" I said as tears rained down my face. I was now in full blown crying mode, tears, hiccups, and snot. "Where is she?"

"Where is who?" Jennifer asked.

"Where is Belinda?" I asked.

"Well, she's in the bed. The EMT's said they were going to call the coroner to come pick up the body," she said.

"You can't let them leave with her!"

"What?!" Jennifer sounded confused, but I needed her to keep Ms. Belinda where she was. If they left with Dom's mom before he had a chance to see her, it would kill him.

"THEY CAN'T TAKE HER OUT OF THAT HOUSE UNTIL ME AND DOMINIC GET THERE! IS THAT UNDERSTOOD?!" I asked.

"Okay, sure. I'll let them know. Are you guys on your way?" she asked.

"Well, as I said before, his wedding is going on right now. I'm gonna have to go to the hotel and pick him up first, then we'll be on our way."

"Okay. I'm so sorry for your loss," she said.

"Thank you."

I ended the call and quickly dried my tears. I didn't know how I was going to break the news to Dominic. All I knew was that I needed to get over to that hotel and pick Dom up. On the ride there, I prayed that he and April hadn't exchanged vows yet. I rushed to get to the hotel and pulled up to the front. I jumped out of my car and got stopped before I could enter the hotel.

"Ma'am, you can't leave your car here unless you're checking in," someone said.

"It's an emergency!" I said and started running. I rushed out through the door that led to the courtyard. The pastor was just about to get the two of them to exchange vows and rings. Thank God!

"DOM!" I called out to him. I could tell by the look on his face that he thought I was there to cause trouble for him, but I really wasn't.

"What the heck are you doing, Rasheeda?" April asked. The sneer on her face made me want to smack the shit out of her, but I had to remember that she was a non-muthafuckin' factor right now. That bitch wasn't shit and thank God I got here before he said, 'I do'.

I waited for Dom to say something, but he didn't. He looked like a deer caught in headlights. "Shut up, April! I ain't here for you!" I snapped at her damn ass.

"Are you really so desperate to keep Dominic that you'd walk up in here to ruin my wedding?" April asked. "You're pathetic!"

"Oh God! Give me the strength to concentrate on the matter at hand. Help me to not lose track of why I came here. Help me to not give in to the temptation to kick this bitch's ass," I silently prayed. "Dom, I've been calling you!"

"Uh, I'm kinda in da middle of somethin'," he said.

"It's your mom!" I said. He rushed over to me, leaving April standing at the altar.

"What's wrong with my mom?"

"We have to get over to her house!"

"Can it wait a few more minutes? We were about ta recite our vows!" he said.

"NOW, DOM! We have to go there now!" I said, my eyes pleading with him to stop being difficult. Couldn't he see that this was about more than his wasted money? This was an emergency involving his sick mom.

He turned towards April and said, "I'm sorry, but I gotta go!"

Tory came rushing over and asked, "Is everything alright?"

"I have to go over to my mom's."

"You want me to come with you?" Tory asked.

He looked past Dom at me and I nodded my head. Shit, he was going to need all the support he could get. "Baby, what's wrong?" a chick who I assumed must have been Tory's girlfriend. It was nice to see he had left that cheating trailer trash bitch alone. He deserved way better than Ashley's ass.

April rushed over and asked, "What the hell is going on here? We're in the middle of our wedding!"

"I have to go!" Dom said as we all rushed out.

"DOMINIC! DOMINIC, YOU BETTER GET BACK HERE AND MARRY ME!" April screamed as we rushed through the double doors leading to the exit.

Dom and I got in my car, while Tory and his girl went to his. I pulled out of the parking lot on two fucking wheels, with Tory following behind.

"What's wrong with my mom?" he asked. He pulled his phone out of his pocket and said, "Jennifer was calling me? I didn't even know."

"Jennifer just said she needs us to get over there as fast as we could," I said as tears clouded my vision. I quickly brushed the tears away and concentrated on getting us there in one piece.

"Why do I have the feeling you're hiding something from me?"

"I don't know."

I looked over at him and he was so damn handsome in that white tux. I turned my attention back to the road. "We're almost there," I told him.

I wanted to tell him what I knew, but I didn't want him to get too upset while I was driving. We pulled up to his mom's house 20 minutes later. The ambulance and coroner's van were parked outside. I watched as his eyes filled with tears. He looked at me and I still had tears in my eyes. I stopped the car and he bolted out the passenger's side. He rushed inside and I followed behind him.

"MOM! MOM!" he called out as he made his way to her bedroom. "MOM! MOM, GET UP! MOM, GET

UP!" I watched as he sunk to the floor, holding his mom's hand. "Mom, you can't leave me! What am I supposed to do without you?!"

I rushed over to him and wrapped my arms around him. He leaned up against me and cried more than I had ever heard him cry before. "She can't be gone, Rah! She can't be gone!"

"I'm so sorry, baby!" I said as I rocked him back and forth.

"Aw damn!" I heard Tory say as he and his girlfriend stood in the bedroom doorway. He came over to where Dom and I were on the floor and said, "I'm so sorry, bro."

Dom was too broken up to respond. A short time later, there was a knock on the entryway. We looked up and the coroner was standing there. He looked at his paperwork and asked, "Who is Mr. Dominic Williams?"

"He is," Jennifer said as she pointed at Dom. That was the first time I noticed her sitting on the sofa in Ms. Belinda's room. She looked broken up and I could understand why. She had been Ms. Belinda's nurse for the past five and a half months. I was sure she had come to care a lot about her.

"Mr. Williams, I am Jarvis Brooks from the coroner's office. I'm so sorry for your loss, but we need to take your mother's body to the hospital now. There are a couple of papers that require your signature, so if you could just sign…"

"You not takin' ma mom nowhere," Dom said.

"Mr. Williams, I promise that we'll take very good care of her…"

"You heard me, man." Dom stood up from the floor and wiped his eyes. "You ain't takin' ma mom nowhere!"

"Can you just give us a minute?" Tory asked.

"Yea, sure."

Jarvis left the room and Tory and I tried to get Dom to let him leave with his mom's body. "Aye bro, da man is just here ta do his job," Tory said.

"Yea baby, he has to take your mom to the hospital," I said.

He sat on the edge of his mom's bed and laid his head on her chest. "Mom, I love you. Please don't leave me. Don't leave Nina. We need you, mom!"

This shit was breaking my heart. I rubbed his shoulders and said, "Baby, your mom needs to go to the hospital."

"NO! I'M NOT LETTING THEM TAKE HER!" he cried.

Tory had tears in his eyes, as did his girlfriend. I didn't know what I could do to get Dom to let Jarvis take his mom. He was now sobbing profusely with his head on his mom's chest. I was crying just as hard as he was. I loved Ms. Belinda and I didn't even get to tell her goodbye. Even though I was sure she knew that we loved her, it would have been nice to have been able to tell her.

"She died by herself!" Dom cried.

"No, she didn't, baby. Jennifer was here," I said.

I looked over at Jennifer and she walked over to the other side of the bed. "Your mom loved you so much. Before she got too weak to speak, she used to brag about you all the time. She called you her little baby making machine," Jennifer said with a smile on her face. "She was so proud of the father you have become."

"I didn't get ta say goodbye," he sobbed. "I didn't even get ta tell her how much I love her."

"Trust me, Dominic, your mom knew how much you loved her," Jennifer said.

He finally raised his head up and kissed his mom on her cheek. "I love you so much, mama."

He got up from the bed and fell into my open arms. Tory came over and wrapped his arms around him also and we cried together. "We're here for you, bro."

"Yea, baby, we're here for you and we love you," I said.

Jarvis came back in and asked, "Are you ready to sign the papers now, Mr. Williams?"

Dom nodded his head. My heart was hurting for him so badly. I couldn't imagine losing my mom. I hated that Dom and little Nina had to go through this. Dom was definitely going to need help raising Nina. I was more than happy to help him with that. He walked over to Jarvis to sign the necessary paperwork for them to take his mom away.

"This is the form that says we have your permission to remove your mom's body," Jarvis explained. "Do you know what funeral home you want us to take her to?"

Dom and I had spoken about this not too long ago, so I answered the question. Jarvis wrote it on the paper and then told Dom where to sign. Once the papers were signed, Jarvis and another man returned with a gurney. There was a body bag on the gurney and I knew that Dom was going to lose it if they closed that bag up while he was in the room. As they loaded Belinda onto the gurney, I watched them. Thank God Jarvis didn't close the bag.

Dom walked over to his mom's body and kissed her cheek again. They wheeled her out of the bedroom and we followed behind them. When it came time for them to close the back door of the van, Tory and I had to hold Dom back. He was beside himself with grief and I was glad that I was here for him. Right after the coroner's van drove off, a car pulled into his mom's driveway. April jumped out and ran over to where we stood. I had my arm wrapped around Dom's waist and his arm was draped over my shoulder.

"DOMINIC, WHAT THE HELL IS GOING ON?!" she yelled.

"I really don't have time for this," he said and made his way back inside the house. Tory followed him inside, but his girlfriend stayed out here with me.

"I don't think you should be here right now, unless you came to comfort Dom," I said.

"COMFORT HIM? COMFORT HIM FOR LEAVING ME AT THE ALTAR? YEA RIGHT!" she yelled.

I stepped up to her and invaded her personal space. She didn't even try to pretend that she gave a shit about what happened. "How about comforting him because his mom passed away?" I asked as I crossed my arms over my chest.

"What?! His mom died?" she asked, finally showing some concern.

"Yes, she did. If you had come here 10 minutes earlier, you would have seen the coroner leaving with her body," I informed her.

"Oh my God! I didn't realize she was that sick."

"Look April, I think that you should just go home and he'll go meet you when he's done here," I said.

"You'd like that, wouldn't you? For me to just leave my man in your clutches, so you could swoop down and seduce him?" she said as she rolled her eyes.

"Wow! His mom just died, idiot! The last thing I'm trying to do is seduce him!"

"You ain't fooling nobody, girl. You've wanted my man ever since you found out about me. Even though our wedding didn't take place today, we're still engaged! That means that he's still mine!" she said as she waved her engagement ring in my face. I wanted to slap the shit out of her for disrespecting me. I wanted so much to tell her about Dom and I, but this wasn't the time or the place. I wasn't even going to stoop to her fucking level because Dom needed me.

"Well, if you're so sure about your relationship, leave. Let him do what he needs to do here and come home to you when he's done," I said.

"Fine! Tell him I'm headed back to the hotel. One of us has to be at the reception to entertain our guests!" she said as she turned on her heels and headed back to her car.

"Wow!" Tory's girlfriend said. "She's some bitch!"

"My thoughts exactly. My name is Rasheeda," I said as I stuck my hand out.

"Krystal, nice ta meet you," she said as she shook my hand.

"Same here. Shall we go back inside and check on our men?"

"Can I ask you something without you thinking I'm being disrespectful?"

Well hell, we just met. If she popped off disrespectful, I might have to pop back.

"Sure, what's up?"

"If Dominic is your man, and he was marrying her, does that mean you're his side…"

Oh hell no! I quickly held up my hand before she could even finish her question. I was nobody's side chick. "Our relationship is complicated. Dom and I have a two-year old daughter together. We actually used to live together, but then we broke up. He got with her and next thing I knew they were engaged. When he found out his mom was sick and that I had been taking care of her while he was away, he started spending time with me. We just clicked, ya know? It was almost like we never broke up. I love him and this morning, he finally admitted that he loved me. Like I said, it's complicated," I finally finished.

"Okay. The only reason I was asking is because I used ta be da side chick," she said.

"Well, now it looks like you're the main chick," I said.

"Yep, and I'm here ta stay," she said.

"Who am I to judge? As long as the two of you are happy, that's all that matters."

We headed back inside and found Dom and Tory chatting with Jennifer. He was thanking her for taking care of his mom. She was definitely an angel from heaven. I wouldn't have been able to do this all by myself. She and I hugged and she said, "Call me if you ever need me."

"I will. Thank you so much for everything," I said.

She said goodbye to us and the four of us sat down and talked until we got hungry. Then we left his mom's house and went to eat at Chili's. Dom was beside himself, but he now knew that his mom was in a better place where she was no longer suffering. We also told him that she wasn't alone because she had Peaches and Slim up there with her, along with her mom and dad. I knew that it would take him a long time to get over his mom being gone, but I hoped that in time, the healing would begin.

Chapter nineteen

Tisha

Four days later...

Hearing that Dominic's mom had died on the same day he was supposed to be getting married shocked the shit out of me. I knew that Ms. Belinda was sick and didn't have long left to live, but I didn't think it would happen that soon. I knew that Dom had to feel horrible about that because I knew how I'd feel if it were my mom. I was under the impression that he and April had gotten married, then found out about his mom. But when I spoke to Rasheeda, she told me that when she got to the hotel, they were about to say their vows. He left before they had a chance to get married.

I knew Rasheeda still loved Dominic and from what I could understand, they were together now. I was happy for her. If Dom was who she wanted and he loved her too, kudos to them. His mom's funeral was scheduled for day after tomorrow and Reggie and I decided to pay our respects to Ms. Belinda. I wasn't going to bring the kids though because three small kids at a funeral was something I hadn't been trained for. I could barely take them grocery shopping because they liked to walk in the store.

We had put the kids in daycare, which worked out perfectly since the funeral was being held Friday morning. At first, I didn't want to put my kids in daycare, but with Reggie and I both working during the daytime, we didn't have a choice. As it turned out, they loved being at daycare. Thank God for small favors.

On this particular day, I was at work when April walked in the door. I just happened to be working the front desk for the receptionist to take her lunch. It shocked me to the point that I almost fell out of my chair. I didn't know what she could possibly be doing here. I looked at the schedule to see if she had an appointment with Doctor Luna, but she didn't. She stepped up to the counter and smiled at me, but I could tell it was fake. I think she had a problem with Dom's babies' mamas because we had his kids before she did.

"Can I help you?" I asked.

"I need to talk to you, privately," she said.

"I'm at work, as you can see."

"What time is your lunch break?"

"What is this about?"

"Dom hasn't come home since his mom died. I don't know where he is or who he's with and I'm starting to worry," she said.

Now, I knew for a fact that Dom was laid up with Rasheeda at one of those apartment type hotels. But I wasn't about to tell her that shit. We weren't friends like that and we definitely weren't allies. After Rasheeda called and told me that Dom's mom had passed away, she also let me in on April's little shenanigans when she went by Ms. Belinda's house to find out where he was. I couldn't believe she was still looking for Dominic to go back to the hotel and marry her. What kind of bullshit was that?

I could understand that no one wanted their wedding ruined, especially before they said 'I do', but damn, his mom passed away. Where was her fucking sympathy for him? Where was her compassion? For that reason right there, I didn't like her ass anymore.

"Humph! Dom hasn't come home and you're doing what at ma job? You think he's wit me?" I asked as I fake laughed. That shit wasn't even funny because I had a man; a good, solid, hardworking man and the best part about loving Reggie was that he loved my children. He loved them so much, they still called him daddy. I picked my hand up and flashed my engagement ring in her face. "Do you see this? This is ma engagement ring dat binds me to ma man. Dom is ma kid's daddy, nothing more, nothing less. So, if he's missing, you should be looking elsewhere. I mean, he does have like five other baby mamas you can check wit."

She stood there as if she was trying to think of something smart to say. "Dom only has four other baby mamas besides you," she retorted. "How did you graduate high school, let alone go to college when you can't even do simple math?"

Oh shit! This bitch was about to make me lose my fucking job. I got up from the desk chair that I was comfortably sitting in and walked around the counter. As I approached her, she looked around like she knew she had fucked up, and she had.

"First of all, I don't fuckin' like you! So, when you start comin' at me wit dat slick talkin' shit, you make me wanna slap da fuck outta you. The only reason I ain't gon' do dat is cuz I'm at ma job, but don't let me see you talkin' dat shit in the streets. I will wipe da flo' wit yo lil monkey ass! Now, when I said Dom had five other baby mamas, dats what the fuck I meant." I picked up my hand and started using my fingers as I named Dom's baby mamas. "Stay wit me while I school yo ass. Rasheeda, Rochelle, Mariah, Ashley, and Shawna. See dat, five, five other baby mamas besides me."

"Who the hell is Shawna?" she asked.

"Duh, Cameron's mom!" I said.

"Cameron? Cameron? You mean the little boy who was the ring bearer in our wedding," she asked.

"Oh wow! Dom let him be the ring bearer in your 'almost wedding'? Dats sweet." I smiled.

"So, you're telling me that Dom has another kid and never told me?"

Wait a minute! Dom never told her about Cameron. Aw shit! I done fucked up with this one, but I'd be damn if I allowed this bitch to see me sweat. I quickly took my foot out of my mouth and composed myself as I smiled at her.

"I didn't know dat you didn't know about Cameron."

"Well, I didn't!" she snapped.

I was two seconds from jumping on her ass, but thankfully, a customer walked in. I rolled my eyes at April and smiled at my customer. "Hello, Mrs. Banks, how are you today?"

"I'm fine, Tisha. It's nice to see you," she said with a smile.

I made my way back to the receptionist's desk and said, "You can have a seat, and we'll call you to the back in a couple of minutes."

"Thank you."

I turned my attention back to April. "I suggest you get the hell up outta here before I forget I'm at work," I said through clenched teeth.

She rolled her eyes and walked out the door. I hated that I had told her something Dom hadn't discussed with her yet, but on the other hand, I was glad I had busted her high and mighty bubble.

*****

The day of Ms. Belinda's funeral was a gloomy and sad one. The weather was nice outside, but that had nothing to do with everything that was about to go down. As Reg and I made our way to the casket, I noticed a couple of Dom's baby mamas were here. I thought that was nice that we came to support him. The only ones who weren't here were Mariah and Rochelle. I didn't know why they didn't come, but that was their business, not mine.

As I stood at the casket and looked down at Ms. Belinda, I noticed how much weight she had lost. She looked so frail and I felt so bad for her. But I felt sorry for Dom the most because he had to be without his mom. I said my prayers, then turned to give my condolences to Dom. I wasn't surprised to see Rasheeda sitting next to him. She had been the one who had been helping him from the start. I was happy for them, that they had found each other again.

About half an hour later, the pallbearers closed Dom's mom's casket and he nearly lost it. His cries could be heard throughout the church. I couldn't even imagine how he was feeling, especially since he was the oldest child. I felt sorry for Dom, but the one I really felt sorry for was Nina. Poor little thing. She was only 18 months old and she'd have to grow up without her mother. My heart broke every time I thought about that. Soon after the casket was closed, April walked to the front of the church and tried to sit next to Dom. The nerve of her coming in after the casket was closed. Stupid bitch!

She really pissed me off because had she cared anything about Ms. Belinda, she would've paid her respects. To have nerve to try and sit next to Dominic. She had another thought coming if she figured Rasheeda was about to move. Rasheeda sat there and mean mugged April's ass, refusing to move from her position and Dom didn't ask her to. Thank God April didn't make a scene because I knew that she would've been dragged out of that church. She found a seat as the services began.

Dom didn't want to have his mom's body at the funeral home because it was only a one day service. That pastor began the sermon as we sat and listened. Then the choir began to sing *Because You Loved Me* by Celine Dion...

You were my strength when I was weak
You were my voice when I couldn't speak
You were my eyes when I couldn't see
You saw the best there was in me
Lifted me up when I couldn't reach
You gave me faith 'cause you believed
I'm everything I am
Because you loved me...

I watched as Dom's body shook as he cried. Rasheeda wrapped her arm around him and held him tight. I imagined she was feeling hurt also. She had been taking care of Dom's mom for a while and the two of them had gotten extremely close. I was glad that the two of them had each other to lean on.

Once the choir finished singing, Pastor John walked up to the podium again. "Belinda Williams was a wonderful woman who would have given her last to help anyone who needed it. She loved life and she loved her children, Dominic and Nina, more than anything. She was a great mother, even though she raised Dominic on her own and was doing the same with Nina. If anyone knew Belinda, she always had a smile on her face. She also was a bit of a firecracker too. You never knew when she was going to let you have it. Dominic, I know that this is hard on you, son, but you have to be strong for your little sister. Your mother spoke to me about you Dominic. When she first found out about her illness, I went to visit her. She loved you so much. She said that she was extremely proud of the way you've stepped up to be the man she always knew you were. She said she had no doubts about you taking care of Nina because you had finally grown up. Her exact words were, 'My little baby maker has finally grown up and learned how to handle responsibility. I know that he will take good care of Nina'. I know the loss of a parent is never easy, especially one as loving as Belinda, but we must never question the Lord. As I look around this church, I can see that you and Nina have a wonderful support system. In time, the two of you will be just fine. You must never forget the smile your mom had on her face every time she saw you. Take comfort knowing that her suffering is over and she is once again happy; no more pain," Pastor

John sat down in his chair and the choir began to sing again.

I recognized the song as *Hero* by Mariah Carey.

There's a hero
If you look inside your heart
You don't have to be afraid
Of what you are
There's an answer
If you reach into your soul
And the sorrow that you know
Will melt away

Tears instantly clouded my gaze as I leaned my head against Reggie. I could tell that Dominic and Rasheeda were crying as well. When that song was over, I stood up and walked to the podium to read the obituary. As I looked out at Dom, he looked so frail and helpless. I guess losing your mom would do that to you. After I finished reading, I felt compelled to say something to Dom. I knew that he was going through something awful, and I just needed him to know that we were all here for him.

"I don't know how many of you know me, but my name is Tisha. Ms. Belinda was my children's grandmother and they loved her so much. I kind of had the feeling something wasn't right with her a few months back, but since she brushed it off as her age and running behind a one year old, I figured that was it. Thank God she had Rasheeda. She really loved you so much, Rasheeda. She considered you her daughter in law." When I said that, my gaze immediately landed on April. I wanted her to know that what Rasheeda did was something her ass should've done considering she was Dom's fiancée. "She once told me that she knew you were the right one for Dominic. She said that she didn't wanna push the two of you together, and that one day, you'd find your way to each other. And y'all did. Dom, I know we haven't always gotten along, but I've always cared about you. You are a wonderful friend and father to our children. I know that this is a hard time for you, but you need to lean on Rasheeda. You two need to lean on each other and as Pastor John said, take comfort in knowing that your mama is no longer in any kind of pain. We love you Ms. Belinda. Fly high like an eagle, honey," I said as I began to cry. I stepped down, went back to my seat, and into the arms of my man.

The services ended 15 minutes later and then we prepared to walk the short distance to the cemetery where Ms. Belinda would be laid to rest. I knew that people often associated funerals in New Orleans with live bands and line dancing, but that wasn't the case here. Walking out of the church, the only sounds we heard were the melodious tunes from the choir as they sang *Amazing Grace*. April brushed past me in an effort to go stand near Dominic. I wanted to snatch that long ass ponytail that slapped me in the face.

She had nobody but the Lord and Reggie to thank for me not doing that. The Lord, because this was his house, and Reggie because he held me back. That was twice she got saved from these hands. The next time, she wouldn't be so lucky.

Chapter twenty

Dom

The next day…

I couldn't believe I had buried my mom yesterday. This past year had been the worst year of my entire life. I had to bury my best friend, then my mom. Thank God for Rasheeda because I didn't know what I would've done without her. Since my mom passed, she had been my rock. I cried on her shoulder as she held me and told me that everything would be alright. She never once turned her back on me or made this about her. Rasheeda was the woman I should've always been with.

I decided it was time to face April and let her know that I wasn't going to marry her. There was no way I could be with her now. She had shown me who she really was this past week. My mom died on the day that she and I were supposed to be married, but all she was concerned about was the wedding. She had blown my phone up that day for me to come back to the hotel, so we could get married. I couldn't believe how selfish she was. Then she made a scene at the dinner that followed my mom's funeral.

She was trying to take the focus off of why we were really there. But Rasheeda wasn't going to let that happen. She asked April to speak with her outside and returned a few minutes later alone. When I asked her what happened, she simply said that she had a talk with April and she left. I didn't believe that for a minute, but I couldn't prove otherwise.

"Babe, are you sure you don't want me to come with you?"

"I told you, I got this. I ain't gon' be long," I said as I kissed her.

"Okay."

I grabbed my keys and left her house. Forty-five minutes later, I pulled up in the driveway of what was supposed to be my home for the long haul. I dreaded having this conversation with April, but I had to do it. For my own peace of mind and hers, she needed to know. Maybe then, she could focus on herself and getting on with her life.

I unlocked the door with my key and called out to her. She came running, but she wasn't happy, nor did I expect her to be. I would have been surprised if she wasn't upset.

"Where have you been?"

"Look April, I didn't come here to argue witchu. I just came here ta talk, but if you insist on arguing, I'm just gonna get ma shit and be out."

"So, you want me to sit down and have a calm conversation with you even though I'm pissed?" she asked.

"Yep, and if you can't, I'm out. I've been through a lot this past week, and I don't feel like arguing witchu," I said. She needed to know that I wasn't going to argue with her and if she insisted on throwing her tantrum, she'd have to do it by her damn self. I had no problem walking in the bedroom, packing up my shit, and leaving without any discussion.

"Fine. I'll do my best to have a reasonable discussion with you."

"Good." I sat down on the sofa and she sat down on the opposite end.

"Where have you been for the past week?" she asked.

"I needed some time ta myself."

"So, you weren't with that bitch, Rasheeda?" she asked with a smirk on her face.

I could've lied to her, but I wasn't going to do that. I was going to be a man about mine and let her know what the deal was. "I was wit her."

"I KNEW IT!" she yelled as she jumped from her seat. "I KNEW YOU WERE WITH THAT BITCH!"

I jumped up from my own seat and said, "Stop calling her dat! She was there for me when you weren't. If it hadn't been for her, I don't know what would have happened to me when my mom died."

"How could you betray me like that? We're engaged. We're supposed to be getting married!" she whined.

"Yea, about dat. The engagement is off," I said.

"WHAT?! You can't be serious!"

"Dead ass! I don't wanna marry you no more," I said.

"What did I do to you?"

"It ain't got nothin' ta do wit what you did ta me. It gotta do wit you not being there fa me. Ma mom was sick, she found out when I was offshore. If you had been checkin' on her and Nina while I was gone, you woulda known she was sick. I'm not blamin' you…"

"Well, it sure sounds like it."

"I'm not. I mean, it ain't your fault ma mom got cancer. I'm just sayin' dat if you checked on her more, you woulda known and you coulda called me," I said.

"You know I was busy planning the wedding and stuff. You don't realize how much goes into planning a wedding," she said.

"You're right, I don't know. But, how much time would it have taken from you ta go check on ma mom. I mean, you didn't even call her once while I was gone."

"I'm sorry about that. I just had a lot going on."

"It's cool. I ain't worried about it no mo. What's done is done," I said.

"When were you going to tell me about Cameron being your son?" she asked as she crossed her arms over her chest.

Damn. I didn't know how she found that shit out, but I definitely didn't know that she knew. "I meant ta tell you about Cameron, but you were always so damn busy."

"Oh please! I would've made time to hear some news like that!" she said.

"It doesn't matter now. I mean, we ain't together no more."

"So, you're leaving me? After everything we've been through, you're just gonna up and leave me?"

"This relationship ain't workin' fa me no mo. I'm just gonna go pack up ma shit and be out," I said as I headed towards the bedroom.

"So, you're gonna walk out on our baby too?" she asked.

That stopped me in my tracks. I turned around to face her because I just knew she had to be kidding. What baby? I used condoms when we fucked. I mean, I may have missed a couple of times, but I remembered pulling out.

"What baby? What are you talkin' bout?" I asked.

"We're having a baby. I was planning to tell you on our honeymoon, but since that didn't happen..."

"You ain't pregnant." I knew she was bullshitting me so I wouldn't leave. I wasn't about to play those games with April.

She walked over to her purse and pulled a paper out. She handed the yellow paper to me. I looked at it and it was a paper from the doctor's office. It had her name and the date on it at the top. I scrolled down and it had the words, 'positive for pregnancy' written on it. My jaw literally hit the floor.

"But how?" I asked.

"I don't know. I just started feeling sick one day, well, the whole week really. I went to the doctor a couple of weeks ago and she said I was pregnant. I'm just as shocked as you are."

I leaned against the wall to keep from hitting the floor. I couldn't believe that shit. How the hell could this have happened? April walked over to me and said, "This baby is a miracle."

Shit! It was definitely a miracle because I definitely wasn't trying to get her pregnant. "Dominic, we owe it to our child to give it a family. That's something you've never had before. Don't you want to stop running so you could give at least one of your children a stable home with a mother and father?"

"Look April, I'll be there fa you during da pregnancy, but I still ain't stayin' witchu. I'm not in love witchu no mo. I care about you, but dats it."

"Woooow! We were just about to get married a week ago, and now, you're standing here telling me that you don't love me. So, if you don't love me, why were you going to marry me?" she asked.

"I could give you $20,000 worth of reasons why I was finna say 'I do'. I'm just glad that we didn't go through wit it."

"Who are you? I don't even know you right now," she cried.

"I'm da same nigga you was wit for da past two years. It's just dat you wasn't there fa me when I needed you da most. A relationship is two people working together, fifty-fifty. Where da hell were you when ma mom died?" I asked.

"You left me standing at the altar!"

"It took you three hours after I left fa you ta show up at ma mom's. What da hell was you doing dat was more important than what I had going on? Oh yea, one of us had ta entertain da guests, right?" She stood there with her mouth hung open. Kind of like mine was hanging when she told me she was pregnant. "Yea, you didn't think Rasheeda woulda told me what you said?"

"Of course, I expected her to tell you. Shit, how else would she have been able to sink her claws into you?"

"Dats da thing though, she ain't gotta lie ta me ta get me. She's always been there fa me. She ain't neva lied ta me," I said.

"So, you're going to leave me to raise our baby on my own?"

"Women do it all da time, but make no mistake about it; I will be a part of my child's life. I will be there fa ma child. I'ma take care of ma responsibility," I said.

She started crying then. I wanted to hug her, but I couldn't do that. I didn't want to confuse her or anything like that. I just walked away and headed to the bedroom. I had taken quite a bit of my stuff over the past couple of weeks while she was at work. I didn't know how she didn't notice that a lot of my stuff was already gone. I grabbed my bags and started putting my things in them. She stood by the doorway in tears. There wasn't anything I could say to her that would make her feel better. She was going to feel the way she felt because this shit was over. I wasn't going to stay with her just because she was having my baby.

Once I had packed my clothes and toiletries, I started putting the bags in the truck. I grabbed my clothes that were on the hangers and started putting them in the truck as well. I'd always care about April, but she wasn't the one I loved. I used to love her, but now I didn't. She was just going to have to get over it. As I put the last of my things in the truck, I removed the key to the house from my key ring. I didn't need it because I was never going to unlock that front door again.

"I love you, Dominic," she said as I handed her the key. "I don't want us to break up."

"I know, but I ain't gon' be witchu just cuz we havin' a baby. Dat wouldn't even be right ta do dat shit. You deserve ta be wit somebody who gon' love you like you deserve ta be loved. Trust me, you gon' find yo special somebody," I said as I gave her a hug.

I lightly pushed her out of my arms after a couple of minutes. "Lemme know when yo next doctor's appointment is. If I ain't offshore, I'ma come witchu."

She nodded her head as I hopped in my truck and backed out the driveway. Since the house was in her name, I was sure her daddy would be more than happy to help her with the bills. That nigga had been wanting to bond with her for a while, but she kept pushing him off. Now, I was sure she'd reach out to him. As I drove towards Rasheeda's place, I felt real good about the decision I made regarding my relationship with April.

When I walked in Rasheeda's house, she immediately took me in her arms. She kissed me on the lips as I held her tight. "You okay?" she asked.

"Yea, I'm just glad ta be home," I said.

"Baby, I love you so much. I just felt the need to say that," she said.

"Thank you fa sayin' dat cuz I needed ta hear it. I love you too."

"That's music to my ears."

"It smells good in here. Whatchu cookin'?" I asked. My stomach began to growl, sounding like a fucking bear. I hadn't eaten since I ate that yogurt earlier. I didn't eat at all yesterday because my stomach was in knots about my mom.

"Just a little crawfish etouffee, some fried catfish, and potato salad. I figured since you hadn't eaten yesterday, you deserved a good meal," she said. This was the reason I loved Rasheeda. She was always looking out for me.

I just held her tighter while I thought about how far we had come.

Chapter twenty-one

Rasheeda

Two months later...

"Well, you are indeed pregnant!" Doctor Miller said as Dom and I sat in her office. I had a feeling that I was pregnant because of the bulge in my belly. I just didn't know exactly how far I was, but judging from my belly, I thought I was at least four months. Things between Dom and I had been going wonderfully, but we had been so busy over the last couple of months that a pregnancy test slipped my mind. When I started gaining weight and feeling these little bubbles in my tummy, I finally admitted to Dominic that I thought I was pregnant.

I had attributed the bubbles in my belly to gas for the past three months. Then when Ms. Belinda died, I thought it was my nerves. But now that my stomach looked like a little mound that reminded me of when I was pregnant with Ari, I decided it was time to visit the doctor. When I asked Dominic to come with me, he was more than happy to accompany me. At first, I was shocked. But when he said that he was always going to be there for me because of the way I had been there for him, it warmed my heart.

After Doctor Miller had given us the news, I looked over at him and he looked happy. I hadn't seen him smile that big since before his mom passed away. "Are you happy?" I asked.

"Yea, I really am," he said as he kissed me.

"Well, I'm going to have my receptionist schedule your ultrasound for a week from now. You look to be between sixteen to twenty weeks, but we'll know for sure once you have the ultrasound done."

"Thank you, Doctor Miller," I said as I hopped off the table. She handed me the chart and Dominic and I walked out of the exam room hand in hand.

The ultrasound was scheduled and we left the building. Once inside the truck, he turned to me and said, "I had no idea you were pregnant. I just thought you were gaining your weight back."

"Wooow!" I said as I playfully punched him in the arm.

"What? I'm being honest. I didn't say anything because if you were gaining your weight back, I didn't wanna seem insensitive. I mean, you gaining weight, but it's cuz you're pregnant!" he said as he laughed.

This Dominic was definitely a totally different person than he was when I had told him about my pregnancy almost three years ago. But, he was 25 now instead of the same immature 21-year old he was then. I was super proud of the man he had become. I leaned across and planted a kiss on his lips. I was oblivious to the fact that April was also pregnant by him. He had given me that news the same night he came home to me after getting all his things.

I loved how we had such an open and honest relationship with each other. We had absolutely no secrets. "Dom, have you heard from April lately?" I asked.

"Nope. I told her ta get in touch wit me fa her next appointment. She ain't holla'ed, so I figured she ain't made da appointment yet," he responded.

"Have you tried to contact her?"

"Nah."

"You mind if I reach out to her?"

"Why would you want ta do dat?" he asked.

"Because you said she only had her aunt out here. Maybe she needs a friend," I said.

I just felt bad for April for some reason. She didn't really have anyone to support her. I just felt the need to check on her since she was carrying Dom's baby.

"So, now you wanna be her friend?"

"Maybe not friends, per say, but just to check on her."

"I guess," he said.

I pulled my phone out and dialed her number. The phone rang so many times, I almost hung up. Finally, after six rings, she picked up. "Hello," she answered.

"Hey April, it's Rasheeda."

"What do you want? If you're looking for your man, he ain't here," she said sarcastically.

Now, here I was trying to be nice. There she was starting bullshit.

"Well, FYI, I'm not looking for my man because I know exactly where he is…"

"Then what are you calling me for?"

"I just wanted to check on you."

"Why would you give a care about me?"

"Look April, I know we aren't friends for reasons we don't need to speak about. That doesn't mean I don't care about what happens to you. I mean, you are carrying Dominic's child, so our children will be siblings. I would hope that the two of us could behave in a civilized manner for the children's sake."

"You don't have to worry about our children being siblings or anything like that because I didn't go through with the pregnancy. I wanted to have a baby by my husband, unlike all you ratchet little hoodrats that don't mind getting knocked up by any man who will have sex with y'all…"

"Hold up now, wait a fuckin' minute! I don't know who the hell you think you're talking to like that…"

"I'm talking to your ass, you homewreckin' bitch! You have a lot of fucking nerve calling me after you stole the man who was supposed to be my fucking husband!" she fussed.

"I think you done lost your damn mind talking to me like that," I said, getting angry.

"Look, as I said, I wanted to have a baby by my husband. I didn't get married, so that means I don't have a husband. Being that I don't have a husband, I aborted that kid. I'm not about to be another baby mama on Dominic's belt. If y'all wanna keep opening your legs and making babies by a man who doesn't care enough to commit to your ass, go right ahead, but I'm not the one. Don't call me again!" she said before she ended the call.

Damn! I pulled the phone from my ear and placed it back in my purse. "I take it that didn't go the way you planned," Dom said.

"No, it didn't. She went off about me being a homewrecker and how your baby mamas are hoodrats. She said that she won't to be one of your baby mamas, so she had an abortion," I said.

"Damn! She had an abortion?" he asked with a surprised expression on his face.

"That's what she said. She said that we were stupid to be having babies by you when you didn't want to commit to any of us."

"Woooow! She on dat bullshit!"

"Well, at least you don't have to deal with her anymore," I said.

I sat quietly as I thought about what April had said. I had a baby by Dominic already and now I was having another one. What would happen to us if he just decided to pick up and leave one day? Not to mention, I had grown attached to Nina and she was attached to me. How would our breakup affect her?

"Rah, don't let what dat girl said get you in yo feelings," he said.

"I'm not," I lied.

"You're lyin'."

He knew me so well. I noticed that we weren't going in the direction of our house. "Where are we going?" I asked.

"I love you and I'm gonna prove it to you," he said.

"Oh Lord! What are you going to do?"

"You'll see."

Ten minutes later, he pulled up into the parking lot to Jared's jewelry store. I looked at him and asked, "What are we doing here?"

"C'mon," he said.

I slid out of the truck as we headed inside the jewelry store. "Hello, welcome to Jared's. How can I help you?" a salesman asked.

"We need a three-piece wedding set," Dom said.

I looked over at him as my mouth fell wide open. "Are you serious?" I asked.

"You love me?"

"Yes," I said with tears in my eyes.

"You believe that I love you?"

"Yes."

"Then I'm dead serious," he said as we walked over to the showcase.

He showed us a bunch of rings, some in white gold, yellow gold and platinum settings. At the end of the day, we settled on a matching set in 14-carat white gold. We had to get the rings sized, but they would be ready in three days. When we left the jewelry story, I was shocked when he pulled up to the courthouse.

"What are we doing here?" I asked him.

"This da only place we can get a marriage license, silly."

"Marriage license? Whose getting married, Dom?" I asked.

"Rasheeda, don't play."

"I'm just saying, you ain't never asked me."

"C'mon, you mean you want me ta get down on one knee and shit?"

"If you expect me to take you seriously."

"But these ma good jeans," he protested.

"Dom!"

"Aight," he said with a smile as he got down on one knee, right there in the parking lot. I knew right then that he really loved me. I was so in love with that man and I couldn't wait for him to ask me to marry him. "Rasheeda, I love you, girl. You gon' make an honest man outta me and marry me? I promise I ain't got no other baby out there and I ain't gon' neva cheat on you. So, you gon' marry me?"

I had to laugh at that boy's antics. He was a fool, but he was my fool. I reached down and grabbed both sides of his face, planting my lips on his. When we parted, he asked, "Is that a yes?"

"YES! YES, BABY, I'll marry you!" I cried as he gathered me in his arms. I knew right then that the two of us were going to make it this time. I had my man and we were getting married.

We went inside and got our marriage license. Four days later, in front of our close family, friends, our little

Nina, and all his babies and their mamas, we got married by Pastor John. I didn't need a big ass wedding, especially after what happened with Dom the first time. He didn't want to cancel the wedding with April because of all the money he spent. Our small wedding and reception costs us only $500, but it was more than I could've ever asked for. I knew that our family was going to make it.

As for Tisha and Reggie, they were getting married in four months, and I was in the wedding as her matron of honor. I was so happy for them. Dom and I were constantly over at their house and they often came to ours. Oh yea, we moved into a bigger place that was in both of our names. Trina was also a good friend of mine. She, Tisha, and I often hung out when Dom was offshore. I mean, why not bond with them? After all, our children were all siblings.

Rochelle, Mariah, Shawna, and Ashley allowed Dom visitation with the kids twice a month. When he was offshore, I still went to pick the kids up for the weekend and Tisha, Trina, and Reggie would help me babysit. Sometimes, Tisha even brought Chrissy, Slim and Peaches' little girl, to join in the fun. It was like a big ass slumber party with the kids twice a month.

Tory and Krystal were still going strong. He had finally found a woman who respected him enough to not cheat on him. She was seven months pregnant, so Keenan was going to have a little sister. Tory and Ashley were able to remain civilized and were co-parenting on a great level. Thank God! Tory and Dominic were still the best of friends. They invited Reggie to join their circle of boys, and they all got along great.

It wasn't easy to get to where we were now. We all had a lot of growing up to do. Good things came to those who waited, and we were living proof of that. I got my man, my family and we got our happily ever after…oh, and little Nina was ours too. As she grew up, we promised ourselves that we'd never let her forget her mama. If it wasn't for Ms. Belinda, I didn't think that Dom and I would have gotten this far. As for that old saying, once a dog, always a dog…well, that wasn't always true. If a man found the right woman to put in his life, and she influenced him to make the right decisions, that dog in him could be tamed.

Any man who had a good woman by his side was capable of change…trust me, I know.

The Real End □□□

Check Out Other Great Books From Tiece Mickens

Presents

Black and Blue

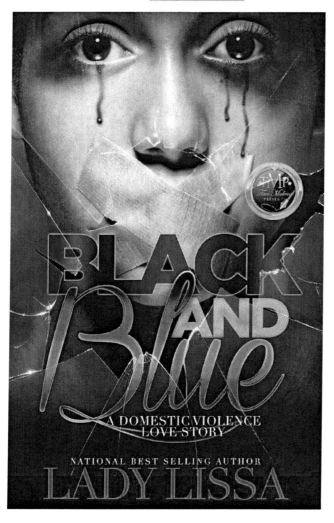

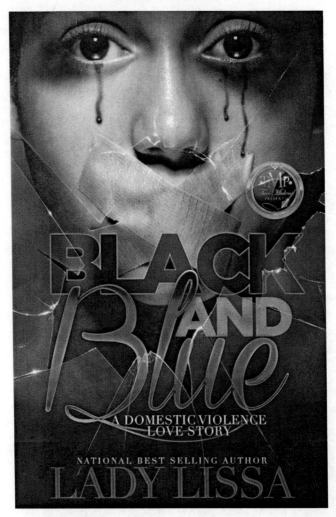

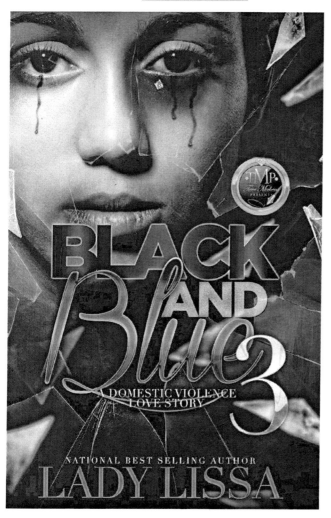

BLACK AND Blue 3

A DOMESTIC VIOLENCE LOVE STORY

NATIONAL BEST SELLING AUTHOR
LADY LISSA

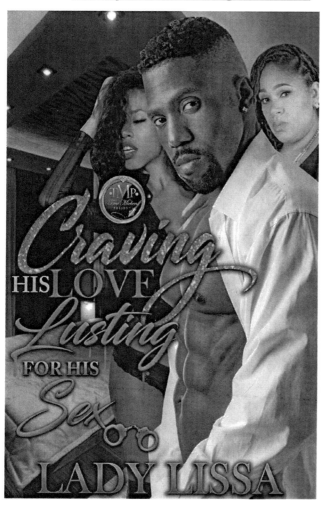

CPSIA information can be obtained
at www.ICGtesting.com
Printed in the USA
LVOW10s2041200318
570524LV00017B/291/P